DRINK WITH THE DEAD

by Jay Flynn

Writing as J. M. Flynn

Black Gat Books • Eureka California

DRINK WITH THE DEAD

Published by Black Gat Books
A division of Stark House Press
1315 H Street
Eureka, CA 95501, USA
griffinskye3@sbcglobal.net
www.starkhousepress.com

DRINK WITH THE DEAD
Originally published in paperback by Ace Books as by "J. M. Flynn" and copyright © 1959 by Ace Books, Inc., New York.

ISBN: 979-8-88601-095-4

Cover design by Jeff Vorzimmer, ¡caliente!design, Austin, Texas
Book design by Mark Shepard, shepgraphics.com
Cover art by Paul Rader
Proofreading by Bill Kelly

First Stark House Press/Black Gat Edition: June 2024

CHAPTER 1

The lights were strong and hot and for too many hours he had been facing directly into the glare, with nothing between but the drifting, acrid layers of smoke. His eyes burned and there was a tight band of pain across his forehead. It wasn't as bad as the one at the base of his skull, where Shannon had cracked him with the .44 Magnum. There it felt as though someone was beating him with a rubber hammer. Forty-five strokes a minute.

The sweating face of Malcolm Tower drifted past the ring of light. Tower was the district attorney's man and his voice was bored, annoyed.

"How about it?" Tower said wearily. He used a handkerchief to wipe droplets of perspiration from his balding head.

"I told you," Jensen said. His throat felt like sandpaper and his tongue was an inch thick. "Shannon tried to run us off the road. Just about scored. I got the car stopped, got the girl out, went after him. Couple of miles further up I saw where he'd gone off the cliff. Wreck was 'way down, already burning."

"So you killed him," Tower insisted.

Jensen's mouth set itself in the stubborn line again. "Find the body. Then come talk some more."

"We'll talk now. I can talk at you for a week if I have to," Tower retorted. Jensen could see the flare of a match as the investigator lighted a fresh cigar. "Okay. We'll get back to the body. Let's talk about why you and McCullough Shannon had trouble to begin with."

Jensen forced a grim smile. "He's the kind of guy you have trouble with."

Tower's big fingers splayed out on the desk behind the lamps. "Two days ago Shannon shot and killed a man in the line of duty. A John Levangie. Supposed to be a photographer. Shot while in the act of burglarizing the Gold Gulch Inn."

"Horse apples," Jensen said. "You give Shannon the routine I'm getting? The hell you did."

"Shut up!" Tower banged a fist on the desk. A paper cup half filled with coffee overturned, dumping its contents on the concrete floor. "You show up in Seacliff claiming to be a private dick. You investigate, which is all right with us. You kill Shannon, which isn't."

"Anything you say," Jensen shrugged. Deep inside himself he enjoyed a silent laugh at the sweat Tower and these other cops were working up. He could make one phone call and walk out of this smelly jail ten minutes later. But that would mean blowing his assignment, if it hadn't been washed out already. When you worked for Treasury under Leonard Purvis, you went by the rules.

Purvis had been FBI before the war. He had been Military Intelligence and later Central Intelligence Agency and finally Agent-In-Charge of the Treasury's Alcohol and Tobacco Tax Unit for Northern California. Purvis' rules said you did not cancel out an assignment by admitting your identity and purpose for any reason.

And Johnny Levangie, who had been a personal friend as well as a good agent, was down in the police morgue with a tag on his big toe.

"Late this afternoon you had a fight with Shannon in the Coast Patrol Service building, Jensen," Tower said. "Tell us about it."

"No fight," Jensen said doggedly. "He got me in there and beat on my head with the butt of a gun."

"*Why?*"

"I didn't ask."

"Tough guy, huh?" Tower came from behind the desk, put his face close to Jensen's again. Jensen could smell the breath heavy with cigar smoke. It seemed to be a particularly vile variety of Italian cigar. "Over the girl?"

"What girl?"

"Rhody Cranston. That big-titted blonde who was in the car with you when Shannon supposedly tried to run you over the cliff."

"Cut it, slob. Refer to the lady like that one more time and I'll break your mouth."

"When? After they take you out of the gas chamber?" Tower laughed scornfully.

"No. Right now. If you think I can't get to you before one of your harness bulls breaks a billy on my head, try it."

Tower straightened up. His fingers strayed to the sleeves rolled tight over his biceps. He was a big man and he scowled at Jensen, then shrugged and stepped back behind the desk.

"We'll let that go for now. She was Shannon's girl, Jensen. But she was out with you."

"She didn't seem to consider herself as such."

"My God!" Tower threw up his hands. He walked away, into the gauzy area behind the desk. Jensen saw the other men in the room draw around him in a circle, heard the suppressed rumble of their voices. He came back, sat his heavy body on the edge of the desk and reached for a Thermos of water. He poured a cup full, held it out. "Like a drink?"

"Thank you. I would." Jensen took the water. He let a few drops slide through his burning lips, sloshed it around his mouth until it was warm before swallowing. He finished the rest of the cup in the same manner.

"More?" Tower asked.

"No thanks. I wouldn't want to feel under obligation."

Tower crumpled the cup, threw it on the floor. "You aren't about to cooperate today. Well, maybe you will tomorrow or the next day. They pay us by the month in this county."

"I'll cooperate. I told you I'd give a statement."

"You don't say the right things."

Jensen shrugged.

"Cop out," Tower said placatingly. "Shannon wasn't exactly popular. The Cranston girl confirms his trying to run you off the road. Tell the truth and a jury'll probably see it your way, Jensen."

"Then why are you working so hard?"

Tower swore. He motioned to a plainclothesman. "Take this dumb Dane upstairs and book him."

"Charge?" Jensen said.

"Suspicion of murder!" Tower snapped. He picked up his jacket from the chair behind the desk and shrugged into it.

"Without a body?"

"We'll find it," Tower promised grimly. "It probably dropped into the river when the car hit that first ledge. Toss anything in that river and it turns up in one of three or four pools."

"Better find it first."

"Thinking about false arrest?" Tower chuckled humorlessly. "We can hold you seventy-two hours on general principles. Even a private dick should know that."

"I know it."

"Then shut the hell up and follow the man upstairs."

CHAPTER 2

Two detectives took Jensen from the basement room where he had been questioned to the third floor, where the booking office was. Two newspaper photographers popped flashbulbs and reporters were pushed back before they could finish their first questions.

The night jailer eyed Jensen, reached into a drawer of the booking desk as he asked, "Any property?"

"Usual stuff," a detective said. He tossed a wallet, handkerchief, keys, small change, comb and pair of sunglasses on the counter.

Jensen leaned on the counter, propped his head in his cupped hands. He blinked his eyes, looked at the items the detective had put down.

"You took a gun away from me too."

"We think that's evidence. You said you cracked off a couple of shots at Shannon with it."

"At his car," Jensen yawned. "Suit yourself."

The detective chuckled. "We will, fellow."

"Charge?" the jailer said.

"En route to anyplace you can think of," the detective replied. "This lad talks like he's made the book before."

Jensen yawned. He wished they would get it over with. He had not had a chance to sleep for a day and a half; he had been beat on by civilians and talked at by cops until he was ready to go to sleep standing up or in any position permitted.

The jailer prodded him in the ribs with a hard finger. "Name?"

Jensen nodded toward the wallet. "It's all in there. Identification, license, the works."

The jailer slapped him on the left side of the face. Jensen stumbled back and sat down hard on a wooden bench placed along the wall. His head rang and he blinked his eyes, trying to focus them. He got his feet under him and the quick rage flooded over the weariness. He was scrambling over the counter after the jailer when the detective rapped him across the throat with stiff fingers.

Jensen choked, clawed at the counter. He slipped off the edge and fell face-down on the floor. A shoe dug into his ribs and he forced himself to lie still.

The jailer leaned over the edge of the counter; a man with a fat, seamed face and white hair. "I want you should tell me. Name?"

He picked himself up. "Konrad Jensen."

"Age?"

"Thirty-three."

"Address?"

"Sea Breeze Motel."

"Occupation?"

"Self-employed."

"Yeah?" The jailer's eyebrows arched. "As what?"

"Put down 'bum,' you fat bastard." Jensen banged a fist on the booking counter. "I told you it's all in that wallet there and as far as I'm concerned you can dig around for anything else you want to know. Now if you want me to go upstairs I'll go and not argue. But keep your goddamn hands off me."

The detectives exchanged pleased looks. The jailer grabbed a sawed-off pool cue from behind the counter and started around it. The detective on Jensen's right grinned and started to peel his coat off.

Jensen dropped to the floor, rolled, came up with his feet braced against the wall and his hands on the wooden bench. He raised it overhead and swung it in a lazy, calculated arc.

It hit the nearest detective on the top of his head. The man fell back against the counter and sprawled flat on his back.

His coat fell open, away from the stubby revolver strapped to his belt. Jensen dove, felt the man's body yield as he landed on it. He yanked the gun out, brought it up to cover the jailer and the second detective.

"Be nice," he said curtly. "Stay alive."

They froze. Jensen flipped the detective's coat back, took his gun. He pulled the pool cue from the jailer's paralyzed fingers. There was an open window at the end of the counter. He backed to it, tossed the stick and the gun out. They clattered on the blacktopped courtyard forty feet below.

The cop who had been hit with the bench groaned and his fingers probed at his head. He sat up, blinked his eyes and looked around the room. He stared at the bench and at Jensen. "Christ! You hit me with that?"

"I did."

"It weighs over two hundred." He sounded doubtful.

"Want me to do it again?"

The detective touched a growing lump on his forehead. "No."

"Then be good."

"Yeah." He picked himself up slowly, watching the gun and the pale eyes of the man who held it. "You busting out?"

"No," Jensen said. He looked at each of them, smiling. "I'm tired. I could use some sleep, and a jail bunk's as good as a four-poster the way I feel."

"Then why …" the detective began.

"Because I don't like being slapped around," Jensen said. "Simple as that. Now, I'll make you a deal. You treat me as a human being and I'll put this gun down and you can take me upstairs and those newspaper guys out in the corridor don't have to know anything about it."

"Oh, yeah?" the jailer said uncertainly.

"I can open that door and let them have a good look at what's going on. I saw a couple of cameras, too."

The detectives and jailer looked at each other warily. The jailer fluttered his hands and muttered, "Oh, hell …"

"Just so we understand," Jensen said. "There are three of you. I can kill or cripple you all … without using a gun. Don't make me do it."

He released the cylinder of the pistol, shook the shells into the palm of his hand and tossed them out the window.

He dropped the gun on the counter, stood with his thumbs hooked in his belt. "Want to go upstairs?"

They hesitated. Then they came, the three moving together. The jailer pressed the button of the automatic elevator and stepped aside. Jensen went in first, walked to a corner and stood watching as the others got in and the small cage moved upward.

They walked him through an outer door. The jailer used a long, flat key on the ponderous door of a tank, slid it back, waited.

"Nighty-night," he muttered, and moved across the threshold.

The jailer tripped him. Jensen cried out, grabbed for the wall, tried to get his footing and his balance. He was bent forward, clutching at the smooth, slick wall when the jailer swung his keys. There were perhaps a dozen on the strap; irregular-shaped pieces of flat, shiny iron about an inch wide and eight inches long.

They struck the side of his head with a clank and a clatter. There was a white explosion in Jensen's brain. The white changed to red as he pitched forward on rubber legs. He felt his face smash on the concrete floor, felt the cartilage of his nose pulp and his lips split, but there was no pain. There was nothing, not even the ability to crawl away from the heavy feet that tore into his kidneys and the hard muscles of his stomach. He could not find the power to curl his legs under him.

He heard a tortured shout, realized it had come from his mouth. He rolled his head, trying to escape the sunburst of pain that was following the explosion. Faces and bodies swirled around him. The jailer was doing the kicking; the two detectives watching.

"Better think up some more answers, Jensen. We'll be back in a few hours with a lot more questions."

Jensen stared at the broad face. He got his arms under him and began to haul himself off the floor. He tried to grin but all he could do was spit blood. He heard the departing rap of footsteps, and the slam of the outer door. He looked around the tank. Jensen managed to sit up. He crossed his legs, got his elbows on his knees and supported his head with his hands. Then he saw the man.

He could have been a bear standing on his hind legs. A balding bear wearing striped boxer shorts. A bear with a moon of a face and a thick-lipped, lopsided grin. The man was about five feet six inches tall but he was the widest man Jensen had ever seen, with practically no neck and knots of muscle all over. Without speaking, he padded over in bare feet, slipped his arms under Jensen's shoulders and picked him up as if he had no weight at all. He carried him into the nearest cell and eased him down on a thin, lumpy mattress. He sat on the opposite bunk and scratched at the thick mat of dark hair that covered his chest.

"Guess you're Jensen, huh?" He had a deep, mellow voice.

Jensen rolled onto his side. There was a sharp pain

in the region of his kidneys and he felt as though his belly had been torn out. He fingered the side of his head. There was a swelling, but the skin didn't seem to be broken.

"Yeah. Thanks. How'd you guess?" He rubbed his eyes and looked around him. The big tank had few occupants. He could see only two other bunks occupied.

"Radio," the bear said. "They let us have one. Said on the late news they'd picked up a guy by that name for a kill. This here's the felony tank and you're the only check-in." He leaned across the narrow space between the bunks, thrust a heavy fist out. "Mayo. Bill Mayo."

Jensen shook the hand. There was a hint of tremendous strength carefully leashed. "Kon Jensen."

"Smoke?"

"Got one." Jensen reached for his shirt pocket, then remembered he'd left his cigarettes at the booking desk. "No I don't either."

"Sit tight." Mayo got up and went to another cell. He came back with a pack of Luckies and a book of matches. "Keep, 'em. I can get more."

"Thanks." Jensen peeled the pack open, offered it to Mayo. They lit up. He drew the smoke deep into his lungs. It seemed like the first cigarette he'd had in years; he coughed, and the coughing brought a fresh surge of pain.

"Hurt bad?" Mayo asked.

Jensen tightened himself, felt the pain subside a little. He took another drag on the cigarette. "I'll be okay. Except for what they did here the cops didn't pound on me. Another guy did earlier."

"Shannon? The one you knocked off?"

"Not guilty."

"Sure. None of us around here are. Particularly me. But the judge says five to life for murder second anyway." Mayo scratched the fringe of hair high on his head and grinned. "Wish they'd take me to hell out of here and up to the joint. I got three months in this bucket and it's all dead time."

Jensen sat and said nothing. He winced as a new throbbing began in his head.

"Hold on." Mayo left the cell again, came back with three small white pills and a cup of water. "Gobble these. Better than aspirin."

"Okay." Jensen swallowed the pills and drank the water. "Haven't got a jug of horse liniment too, have you? That's what I'll need in a few hours."

"Nope. Good rubdown should fix you up, though. I'm a masseur. Lay you out on the table there and pound on you awhile. Really fix you up."

"Then I can hurt all over instead of just in spots." Jensen yawned, shut his eyes.

"Do you good. No kiddin'." Mayo stood, flexed his huge biceps. "Guess you wanta sleep. How about breakfast? They feed at seven. Not worth wakin' up for."

"If it's a case of eat at seven or don't eat, I guess I do. They promised me another trip to the room downstairs."

"Hell, forget it. They let us send the trusties out for chow. Get about anything you want from a hash house down the block. I got some dough and won't have any place to spend it in a couple more days when they take me up."

"There's a couple hundred dollars in my wallet downstairs."

"Then you can sign chits." He flicked the butt of his cigarette to the floor and crushed it with a bare foot. "Get some sleep." He went back to his own cell.

"Sure. Thanks." Jensen finished the cigarette. He took his sports shirt off and stretched out on the bunk. He wondered about the time and supposed it was between four and five in the morning.

He could feel the pills start to take effect. He closed his eyes and wondered if Leonard Purvis knew yet how he had bitched things up, and if so what he was doing about it.

Purvis probably knew, because Mayo had said his name was on the radio. Purvis was probably doing nothing until he could find out the details. And at the present stage, Purvis would probably continue to do nothing; leave Jensen in jail until he could figure a way to get himself out.

Jensen considered it. He could call some local lawyer and have him try for a writ of habeas corpus. He imagined this would take several days. He didn't intend to spend that much time in a cage while the people he was looking for went about covering themselves.

So far they had done a good job. Not good enough because Johnny Levangie had obviously turned something up; something which had cost his life.

Jensen had worked two days without much in the way of results. He had managed to get himself jailed because the law thought he had killed a door shaker named McCullough Shannon.

The bureau really wasn't much farther along than it had been the day the Highway Patrol captain had walked into the office and dropped a heavy briefcase on the desk of Leonard Purvis.

That had been just two days after a truck which had been loaded with whisky tumbled down a mountain eighteen miles north of Seacliff and burned.

CHAPTER 3

It was a day of gray shadows in San Francisco, with the winter rain slanting down, hissing in the steep gutters; the fat, heavy clouds bunched on the hills of Marin County across the turbulent, whitecapped water. Cable car gripmen swore at the slickness of the tracks. And the bars in the big hotels around Union Square and on Nob Hill did a good business.

The office was bleak and functional and one of the panes of glass in the left-hand window was cracked and leaked a little. A steam radiator hissed and spat its discontent. In years past it had left its mark on the yellowish plaster walls. Two overhead lights cast a yellowish light that came close to matching the shade of the walls. There were a few golden oak desks and wooden chairs; not new, because the Alcohol and Tobacco Tax Unit of the Treasury Department is not a high-budget agency to begin with and the men who staff it spend most of their working days or nights in the field. Besides the desks there was a large wooden table which was the fountainhead of activity. A game of double-deck pinochle was being played around it and an electric coffee pot gurgled at one end.

Leonard Purvis' long face grew longer as he arranged the cards in his hand. He had three legs of a double pinochle and if Matty could come through with the other leg it would be free lunch today.

"Cards are just about like the weather," he said dolefully, eyeing the score sheet kept by Levangie, on his left. His face bunched up around his smoldering pipe; a face of prominent bones, wide, deep eyes and too-large features. "Pretty bad."

"Worse than having no cards at all," Matty agreed. She sucked her plump cheeks in tight against her teeth.

"Got any dough, Lev?" Jensen asked.

"Nope." Levangie rocked back in his chair. He was, a tall, angular man with big hands, coal-black hair and bushy eyebrows. His necktie had crawled up under the right tab of his collar again. "Who needs money when he works for Uncle?"

"Well, the boss and the office girl sure haven't needed any this week." Jensen folded his cards. "Partner, I got a low suspicion we're the big spenders again today."

"Entertaining the boss is deductible," Purvis said.

"I put down on my return I'm entertaining you and the boys over at Internal Revenue will fix us up with a branch office at McNeil Island," Jensen said. "I could go knock over a bootlegging cabbie I've been saving for a slow day and—"

He was interrupted by the buzzer which sounded as the door to the outer office opened. Matty shoved her glasses up on the bridge of her nose and went to investigate. She was back in a moment, picking up her cards as she said, "Live one. State patrolman with some hot stuff. He thinks."

"Show him in," Purvis said. He stood, swung around

to face the door. He had come out of the war a brigadier general and he was an erect, imposing figure.

Jensen and Levangie got to their feet as a stocky man in a gray business suit and hat of matching shade came in. He carried a raincoat across his arm, and a briefcase which he put on the big table. It thumped heavily.

"Dean Searle, Highway Patrol Captain in Rio de Oro County," he said, shaking hands with Purvis. "Got something for you to look at."

"Johnny Levangie and Konrad Jensen," Purvis replied. "What's your problem?"

"This is no problem for me," Searle said. He opened the briefcase and removed two bottles, placed them side by side on the table. They appeared to be unopened bottles of a nationally advertised straight bourbon whisky. "If you fellows say they're okay, I'll take care of them myself. Couple of nights should do it."

Purvis smiled. He leaned over the table, eyeing the bottles closely, not touching them.

"If you're thinking about fingerprints, there weren't any," Searle told him. "I grabbed this stuff myself and first thing I did when I thought something might be phony was dust them."

"Good thinking," Purvis told him. He stepped aside as Jensen brought a magnifying glass, a looseleaf binder and a pair of dividers.

Jensen picked up the nearest bottle, inspected the bottom, flipped through the binder to the catalogue of distillers' bottling marks. He compared the design blown into the base of the bottle and the numbers on it with the book, nodded and ran his tongue along his lower lip. He turned more pages, studied the labels and the tax stamp across the cap.

"Uncle never got his ten bucks a gallon on this," he said with finality. "Fine counterfeit. But the bottler code's wrong and there are some flaws in the labels and stamp." He turned to Searle. "How'd you come to figure the stuff's bootleg?"

"The circumstances involved were—" he began.

"Excuse me," Purvis interrupted. "We'd better get your story down on the recorder."

Levangie brought a dictating machine, adjusted the stylus over the plastic belt, turned the microphone on and rapidly spoke into it the time, date, subject of the interview and the names of those present.

As he spoke, Jensen took a tiny electric-powered drill from a desk drawer. He bored a hole through the bottle cap, poured a small amount of the contents into a sterile container, melted a gob of sealing wax and closed the hole, pressing his thumb down firmly on the hot wax.

"We can proceed now, Captain," Purvis said as Jensen pushed a plastic stopper into the neck of the specimen bottle, sealed it and wrote his name and the date on its label. "But first, have you had lunch?"

"Not yet. I'm not hungry at the moment," Searle replied.

"This may take longer than you think. I'll have some

steak sandwiches sent in." He nodded at Matty, who picked up a phone and dialed. "Mr. Jensen and Mr. Levangie, who are excellent investigators but horrible pinochle players, will pay."

Jensen and Levangie scowled at the score sheet.

Searle chuckled. "Fine. Well, I'll give you what I think is essential and from there on you can pick my brains." He took a leather-bound notebook from his jacket, consulted it. "At 8:39 P.M. on December 10, which was just two nights ago, I was patrolling Highway 11 about twenty miles north of Seacliff. That's a mountain road, extremely steep, with many short-radius turns. It follows the northwesterly wall of the valley, along the side of a steep slope. The mountains run up more than four thousand feet. The drop into the valley and the river, which is to your right as you go away from Seacliff, is anywhere from two hundred to two thousand feet. In some places the wall is heavily forested. Others it's mostly brush, and there are some stretches where there's nothing but rock.

"It's a secondary road. When you hit the summit you can go on to San Jose or San Francisco. Traffic is moderate to heavy in the tourist season but I don't imagine it's used more than ten times a night at this time of year. I came on a parked car on the opposite side of the road, headed toward Seacliff. I put a light on it and saw it was occupied by three male juveniles, apparently asleep. I walked up to it, rapped on a window and opened the driver's door. There was a strong odor of whisky. Two of the boys had vomited on themselves and the inside of the car. I radioed for a tow truck and another Highway Patrol officer. Am I going into too much detail?"

"You're doing fine, Captain," Purvis said.

"Good enough. Well, then I tried to get the boys to wake up. It happens I know them and I was somewhat surprised. They'd never been in trouble before. It took me some time to bring them around. I managed to get them out of the car and walking around in the road to sober up. Patrolman D. J. Green arrived and we went through their car. We found a bottle the same as those on the table under the front seat. It was empty. In the trunk we found three cases of the stuff. One case open with a jug missing. I figured they'd broken into some place or other and had Green put them in the back of his patrol car. I questioned them there."

"The remainder of the whisky, Captain? Where is it?" Purvis asked.

"In my personal custody. From what I discovered in the next couple of hours I thought it might be more than a routine burglary. Something that should be kept quiet."

"Good. It's exactly as you found it?" Purvis said.

"Except that in the presence of Officer Green I opened the two sealed cases, photographing them and their contents. I sealed them, Officer Green and I both wrote our names and the date on the tape and he witnessed me putting them in a locker and both locking and sealing it with the type seal used on railroad cars. I have the only key."

Jensen whistled softly. "Not taking chances, are you."

"The Patrol has rigid procedures on caring for evidence," Searle said. "We try to anticipate defense attorneys."

"I suppose the kids had a story," Jensen said.

Searle lit a cigarette. "They sure did, and it sounded pretty wild at first. Denied breaking into any of the summer places or a liquor store. Claimed to have bought it off a guy but as usual didn't know who he was. We broke them of that tale pretty quick. Said then they'd just been driving around earlier and came on this truck a few miles on up the road. Claimed it had clobbered a big redwood and there was nobody around. They got the van open and found it full of booze, decided to help themselves, which they did. Thought it would be a good idea to sample a little while they figured out what to do with the stuff now that they had it. The problem was all taken care of by the time they woke up. The tow truck came about then and Officer Green and I took the kids up to where the truck was supposed to be."

The door alarm rasped. Matty went out and returned in a moment with a cardboard carton. The smell of steak filled the small office. She dug into a drawer for eating utensils, brought cups from a locker and shut the recorder off.

"Dig in, boys. And somebody pony up about eight bucks." She waited with outstretched hand, looking from Levangie to Jensen and back again.

"Four more you owe me, partner," Jensen said as he counted out money from his wallet.

"And we do admire a big spender," Matty said as she went to pay the messenger.

They ate leisurely. The day outside grew darker and the rain fell in a steady torrent so they could no longer see the heaving surface of San Francisco Bay. When they were finished and smoking cigarettes, Purvis went to a cabinet and brought a bottle of dark rum to the table. There was no tax stamp on it. He spiked the coffee liberally.

"Liberated by our agents in Florida," he told Searle. "Top Cuban stuff, hundred fifty-one proof."

"Gawdalmighty!" Searle said after taking a swallow. "I'd better get on with my story while I can still talk."

"Please," Purvis said. He turned the recorder on.

"There was no truck, but there were signs that a vehicle of some kind had hit the tree and had been dragged away. There were faint tire marks left by at least one other vehicle, apparently a fairly heavy truck with duals on the rear. The drag marks went to the edge of the cliff. It looked as though someone had pushed the damaged vehicle over. The kids were still pretty drunk but they swore they hadn't done it, which we never thought they did in the first place. They couldn't remember what time they'd grabbed the stuff. Just that it was dark, which would have made it some time after 4:30 P.M. We took a look down the canyon but there was nothing to see. Impossible to go over the side at night, so we had to wait for daylight. We questioned the boys, concluded there was no more they could tell us so I took them to their homes. I told their families some white lies and asked them not to punish the boys until we'd investigated some more. And not to talk about it. They grabbed at a chance to keep people from knowing their lads were drunks and thieves."

"There's been nothing in the papers?" Purvis asked.

"Nothing. We didn't log the case."

"You can come to work here any day you want, Captain," Purvis told him. "What's the rest of it?"

"Green and I went for a look the next morning. Had to walk in a couple of miles along the river. We found chunks of truck strewn from hell to breakfast. It was pretty much burned up. A one-ton Chev. We took down the motor number, found the rear license plate. The plate was a fake and the motor was out of a wagon that had been junked a couple of years ago at Fresno. I doubt we'll ever trace it. Looks like they figured it was better to dump the thing rather than take a chance on having some officer spot them towing it in and ask questions."

"Too bad," Jensen said. "If we had some idea of where he picked up his load there'd be more to work with. He could have been running the ridges from some place hundreds of miles away."

"I'm reasonably certain it came from the county," Searle replied. "Green and I climbed a good way up the face of the mountain. We found parts of the truck but no sign of a whisky bottle. Not one. However, we picked up a cash receipt for service and a little better than forty gallons of gas on the truck. The driver must have had it in the cab and it spilled out on the way down." He produced an envelope and took a yellow form from it, spread it on the table. "This shows a lube job was done on the truck that afternoon, by the Seacliff Truck Stop. They noted the mileage. I checked the odometer on the wreck and it showed just fifty-six miles more than this. Now, no matter which direction you take, you can't get out of the county in that distance. Unless you drive into the ocean."

"We can start with the garage, then," Purvis said.

"I think your work's all done for you," Searle replied. "We talked to the attendants. They remembered the truck and are sure it was empty at the time. The driver was about five feet eight, on the thin side, wore work pants and a cloth jacket. With dark glasses that covered the upper part of his face and a cap so they couldn't say what color his hair was, except that it showed some gray at the temples. He was a stranger and he paid cash. That's about it."

"It's a better lead than we usually get, Captain," Purvis said. "Excellent police work, which is something we rarely find. We normally try to work without bringing local authorities into a case."

"Meaning you don't get the cooperation you need?"

"God, they cooperate us to death," Purvis told him. "We have to work undercover or our birds fly. The average police officer wants to put the arm on anybody that looks likely, which is fine when you're hunting for a burglar or car thieves, that sort of situation. It's murder for us."

"Well, call me if you need me. Glad I could help." Searle picked up his hat. "I'd be interested to know how this turns out."

"I can tell you this much, Captain," Purvis said as they shook hands. "It'll be big. We can guess that much just by seeing the bottles."

"Oh?" The patrolman looked at them with new interest.

"Well, there's the glass itself. Except for a few small flaws, it's a skillful replica of this company's own bottle. Manufactured expressly for the distiller. We know exactly how many are ordered and delivered and we have an inspector at the plant to observe the filling and other processes. We know to the drop how much whisky he should get from a given quantity of raw material. If he's over or under, he's in trouble. The bottle maker wouldn't sell to you; he'd string you along and tip us off."

"Any whisky bottle I buy has whisky in it," Searle said, grinning.

"So do those, now. We'll know what it's made from and how old it is after the lab gets through," Purvis explained. "Meanwhile, there are the stamps and labels. Not a problem for a bootlegger like the bottles, but they still require a small printing plant and the use of a skilled engraver to make the plates. An outfit big enough to turn out steam that just looks this good has to have plenty behind it. While I think of it, have you smelled anything like a still down there?"

"I wouldn't know one if I did."

"They smell pretty bad. Yeasty, sort of sharp and sour," Purvis told him.

"Then I haven't smelled one. But that's a lot of territory. Better than a thousand square miles in the county, and except for the shore line most of the citizens are cows or lumberjacks. There was a little mining years back, but it never amounted to much. Terrain is pretty rugged."

"I've been there a few times," Purvis said. "Thanks again. One more thing, before you go. I don't believe I have to mention it, but you never saw Jensen and Levangie. They'll be moving in fast, probably with other agents, in cover jobs. They sometimes get in trouble, in which case it's up to them to get out as best they can."

"I understand," Searle said. "Even Green doesn't know I came here."

"Good. From what you've told us, our pigeons may not suspect anything. They probably think somebody came along and helped himself to a few cases of the stuff and then got the hell out. This is fine if it's true—the cooker will be a lot easier to find if it's still running," Purvis said.

"Sure. Well, good hunting, men." Searle shook hands with Jensen and Levangie and started for the door. He paused, slapped his briefcase against his leg and looked at the bottles. "Is there really a lot of that stuff around?"

"You better believe it, Captain," Purvis replied. "Suppose this comes from a fair-sized still, one that turns out, say, a thousand gallons for every twenty-four hours it operates. Maybe two hundred days in a year's time. That costs Uncle better than two million dollars in taxes."

Searle whistled softly.

"Nobody really knows how much 'shine is being turned out. Most of it is horrible stuff but occasionally some of it could get by on the legitimate market. Our best guess is that at least a third, possibly a half, of the liquor manufactured in this country last year never saw a tax stamp." Purvis paused to tamp tobacco into his pipe and get it going. "Maybe a billion dollars in taxes lost. And even today, that's a lot of bucks, Captain."

CHAPTER 4

They stared at the closed door in silence. Then Jensen refilled his coffee cup and added more rum. He lit a cigarette, blew on the steaming drink and said, "Guess I'll go pack."

Levangie stood, examining a bottle. "Let's not get grabby. I might like to get out of the city for a while myself."

"I thought we'd both go."

Purvis relit his pipe. "Let's not ride off in all directions at once without mounting our horses first," he said. "Matty, see what we have in the files on Rio de Oro County."

They watched her broad rear as she bent over the bank of filing cabinets. She checked several folders and brought them over. "There was some action down that way in Prohi days. Apparently the fishermen working out of there were bringing stuff in from Mexico and Canada. Since then, not a thing but a couple of Italians picked up for making grappa—that was nine years ago—and a guy brewing beer in his garage. Neighbor kids got in and one of them was cut up by an exploding bottle, otherwise there probably wouldn't have been a kick. Interested?"

"Hmmmm ..." Purvis made smoke rings from the bowl of his pipe. "List the names and addresses, just in case."

"Didn't they have some kind of political flareup down that way a couple of years back?" Jensen asked. He took his coffee and went to the window, watching the rain. It showed no sign of diminishing.

"Matter of fact they did. Nothing to concern us, but there was some big squeal over pinballs and girls. Wound up kicking some boy district attorney out. But that gives me an idea." He went to the phone, dialed, spoke quietly and rapidly into the mouthpiece. When he hung up, he said, "The attorney general's lads were on that one and they've got a file with a lot of interesting names on it. I'm going to amble over and see Robbie. You guys find something to do and I'll check in here with you in a couple of hours."

He put on his hat and raincoat and went out. Levangie stared glumly at the rain and said, "Squarehead, can you think of anything we can do here?"

"Nothing the General would approve of."

"Then I guess we get wet."

"Our leader is getting wet." Jensen finished the hot coffee and took his hat and coat from the rack inside the door. "I'll drop the sample by the lab and call on a few wholesale houses, see if I can get an idea how deep this operation is cutting and what brands are off when they shouldn't be." He turned to Matty. "I'll need sales figures by brand and distillery for domestic whiskies over the last couple of years. Federated Institute should have them."

"Yes, dear, I know," she said, tongue-in-cheek. "Just

California or the whole Coast?"

"Better make it nationwide. I doubt this stuff's moving off the Coast but I want to know if a brand's dropped off just here or all over. An outfit like this could be faking a couple of dozen labels." He headed for the door.

"So what's that leave me?" Levangie demanded.

"What you usually grab before somebody can beat you to it. The cat houses, bottle clubs, cabbies. I'm wholesale, you're retail." He pulled the door shut and quickly left the building.

The laboratory was a maddening two blocks distant—too close to make a cab worthwhile and too far to walk and keep the feet dry.

Jensen shook the water from his hat and heard his feet squish in wet shoes as he went into the office. A technician in a white smock came from a rear door and Jensen gave him the bottle.

"We want to know as much about this stuff as you can possibly tell us. If there was an ounce of Old Horse in the mash, we want to know what color he is."

The technician began filling out a form. "Couple of days okay?"

"Couple of hours."

"Can't, pal. Be four hours anyway. Means overtime."

Jensen got a cigarette out and fished for a match. "Work overtime then."

"Hot, huh?"

"Yes, dammit. She's got red hair and green eyes and

beaucoup cleavage and I want to know if this stuff will melt the lock off her chastity belt, Horatio. Get with it."

The technician backed away toward the door through which he had entered and retorted, "Okay, T-man, okay. Whatever the rules are. And I'm Harold."

"Fine, Harold. I'll be back."

He splashed back out in the rain.

He tilted his hat back and let the rain lash his face as he walked up toward Union Square. There was a small bar a half-block from the square where he approved of the Irish coffee. He went in and found it almost deserted. It was the slack time between the late lunch drinkers and the cocktail hour.

It was a mellow taproom, with the smell of good leather and warm, intimate shadows. The white-haired barman looked up from the board where he was cutting up the garnish for the cocktail trade and said, "Hi, Kon. The usual?"

"Right, Chub. And it's no fit day for a poor man to be walkin' the streets, so bear it in mind."

The barman spooned sugar into a glass, added dark coffee from a silver urn, injected Irish whisky and spooned rich whipped cream on the top. He placed it in front of Jensen as a cocktail waitress came from the rear of the room to the station beside him.

She was a full-bodied girl with fair skin and a pretty face. She had chestnut hair and green eyes, and her man-style blouse and the simple black skirt gave her an air of controlled sensuality. She slid her serving tray across the bar, studied Jensen's face for a minute and said, "You're going to go mysterious on me again."

"Hi, Collie," he said, smiling. "What's that mean?"

"Broken dates. Usually some lumps on your head. And utterly no explanation." She grinned. "I think you do it to fascinate me."

"Hasn't done me much good so far. Drink?"

"Keep trying. I think I'm beginning to weaken." She looked around, counting the empty booths. "Guess I could squeeze one of those in."

Chub made her an Irish coffee and set up a second one for Jensen. Collie Fitzgerald sipped it and licked traces of whipped cream from her lips.

"Know any call girls?" Jensen asked.

She lowered her glass carefully to the bar and he saw the green eyes begin to smolder. "If I thought you meant that …"

"I know. You might weaken to save me from the well-known fate. It's business. I may need some information in the next few days, Collie."

"What sort of information?" She pursed her lips thoughtfully. "Kon, they haven't put you on the vice squad?"

"I'm not that kind of a cop. More than that you don't have to know. This is for real. I need to talk to some call girls or party girls or both. Can you fix me up?"

"I don't understand why you think I'd know any. This isn't a tenderloin dive."

"No. But I can stand on the sidewalk in front of the place and hit some of the biggest office buildings and stores in San Fran with rocks. Those places are loaded with girls and a lot of them come in here. I don't say they're all doing piece work at night, but some of them are."

"I think that may be why I can stand you off, Kon. Because it might be just piece work to you." She drained her glass and set it down hard on the bar. "Sure, a lot of girls come in after work. I hear bits of conversation, and often one of them will use the phone and then go wait in a booth. Sooner or later there'll be a man in the booth. For all I know it's her husband."

"Except it's a different husband all the time, which is beside the point. Look, I'll narrow it down a little more. It's not the girls but the guys they go out with I'm interested in. I want really to talk with a few big-spender types. Ones that toss parties and talk about getting stuff wholesale because they know a man. I have to find them through their women."

"Ha!" She tossed her dark hair and laughed softly. "Now we get to the point. You are looking for a man. A man who sells things wholesale. What did he steal and where can I buy some?"

Jensen sighed and wondered if he would ever be able to pick a woman's brains without finding his own skull empty first. He wished he had something nice and simple, like being an inspector in a homicide division. Homicide inspectors just went around asking questions and peering at bits of evidence and making deductions and sooner or later they came up with an answer of sorts. There was nothing secret about that line of work. Every move was reported in the papers. Often before it was made.

He couldn't operate that way. He could, but if he did he'd never catch anything except hell from Leonard Purvis. He couldn't even tell this long-legged Irish girl whom he liked and trusted and occasionally tried to sleep with what his job was. She knew only that he was some kind of peace officer. A dog catcher is a peace officer. He gets to carry a gun.

Jensen decided to tell a half-truth and stick a lie on top of it.

"He stole some whisky in Illinois. From a warehouse, a particular, isolated warehouse. Nearly three thousand cases." He signaled Chub for two more drinks. "It looks like part of it is here on the Coast, and there's no more hard-drinking place than San Fran."

"Three thousand cases!" She shut her eyes and did some mental arithmetic. Even mediocre blends retail for more than fifty dollars a case. "That could be two hundred thousand dollars!"

"It could be a hell of a lot more than that, honey. That stuff was condemned. Contaminated."

"I don't understand … If it was bottled …"

"It was a freak thing. The Atom people popped one of their toys in Nevada. Prevailing winds carried the fallout over the Plains states. Came down right on these wheat fields that were under contract to a distillery. It was a big bomb and a dirty one. The grain was contaminated but nobody knew it at the time. So they cooked it up and put it in bottles. Found out last year what had happened."

"My God! Could it kill a person who drank it?" Her eyes, wide with sudden apprehension, moved over the glittering rows of bottles on the back bar.

"One bottle wouldn't. The radioactivity isn't that potent. But if a guy was to buy enough of it, he could get seriously ill. Possibly die, depending on his physical condition—and most heavy drinkers aren't in good shape."

"But there hasn't been a thing in the papers. Why don't they publicize it?"

"That would do what Volstead couldn't. Ruin the liquor industry. Put a million people out of work—and for what? The way it is, only the guy who chisels is going to get hurt. If we said it just happened to one brand, you know what he'd do? Take the labels off and call it something else." Jensen paused, somewhat awed at the monster he had created. He shrugged. "Even being radioactive, it's not as bad as bathtub gin used to be, or some of the cheap sugar alky they still boil up in the dry states. But we'd just like to get the stuff back."

"Yes. Well …" She pushed the Irish coffee away from her.

"Drink it. It cost a buck and there's not a darned thing wrong with Irish whisky. The cloud didn't get that far."

"All right. I'll see what I can do."

"Discreetly, or you'll start an avalanche of bottles

rolling down Telegraph Hill to the Bay."

"Sure." She tried her drink. "Kon, I'm thinking of what might be a better idea."

"Oh?"

"I was holding back a little before. I do know several girls who make a steady thing of these wild parties. They come in and tell lies to each other about how much liquor there was or how many went swimming nekkid in the moonlight, you know. I could just say we heard in the trade that a new tax is going to be slapped on and I'd like to put a few aces by. I'll bet two or three say they know a guy who knows a guy who can get it cheap."

"No," Jensen said firmly. "It could be trouble for you."

"Pooh!" She swung a long, nyloned leg from the bar stool. "I'm not going to go sneaking down back alleys to meet anybody. I'll just find out who to see and my boyfriend can go with me."

"Boyfriend?" He eyed her sharply. "Let's bring the whole family."

"I mean you, idiot."

"Oh. Well, give it a try. Don't do any more than ask."

"I might know something later tonight. I'm off at eight."

He grinned. "I'll be here about then."

He left the car and walked down to the garage under Union Square. The attendant brought his two-year-old coupe and he drove across town to the warehouse and office of the largest liquor wholesaler in the city. He parked in the lot beside it, sidestepped mud puddles and went into the office, where he waited while the manager was paged. He was studying a picture of the firm's first distillery when the door opened.

"Damn it, you just audited us three weeks ago." The manager grinned and shook hands. "What's up, Kon?"

"Hi, Kemp. We just counted the cases before. Thought it might be good to open them up and see if there's anything inside."

"I knew if I waited long enough something worse than the rain would show up." He went behind the broad, glass-topped desk and dropped into a leather-upholstered swivel chair.

"Yeah. Say, how's Ancient Vulture going lately?"

"That's no way to talk about our best sippin' whisky." Kemp swung around, got a heavy binder from a rack behind the desk. "Really want to know?"

"Yeah. And the reason?"

"I smell something. I was about to start smelling something anyway." He flipped pages. "Don't tell Seagram, but we're down almost ten percent from what we were last year at this time. That's a hell of a lot, when we should be up."

"Why?"

"Absolutely no reason that I can see. No more hot competition than it ever had, and plenty of advertising. Vulture is holding its own in the bars, and so are most of our other labels. The package store volume is what's gone to hell."

"Just Vulture?"

"No. From our figures it looks like people have just about quit drinking bourbon and blends at home. We know pretty well what the other guy sells and they're all hurting. In the stores, mind you, not the bars."

"Switch in taste, maybe? More vodka or Scotch."

"Oh, hell." Kemp studied the statistics. "Vodka's doing better and so are gin and Scotch. Liqueurs have taken a big jump but that's from advertising and they're small spuds anyway. Just no legitimate reason for it."

Jensen prowled the office. "How about an illegitimate reason?"

Kemp shrugged in futility. "Hell, you always hear things. Half a dozen times a year you guys knock over a 'shiner. What comes out of those backyard rigs would kill a musk ox. But it couldn't hurt Vulture or any other whisky fit to drink."

"So what have you heard?"

"Vague rumbles of a discount deal. If there was anything worth repeating I'd have been sitting in your office as fast as I could get there, Kon."

"What kind of discount?"

"I can't find out and my salesmen can't find out. Just that a few package dealers said the stuff isn't moving because some of their big customers who used to buy cases at a time quit cold when the dealer wouldn't sell them Vulture at forty bucks a case. Hell, the dealer pays sixty to us and has to make a profit on top. State law won't allow discounts anyway."

"Tell you what." Jensen studied a woodcut engraving

of the original Vulture distillery. "Talk to your salesmen in the next couple of days. If they can remember which dealers came up with this rumble, have them try to find out which customers are involved. We'll go talk to a few of them before you go bankrupt."

"Yeah. I'll do that." Kemp made notes on a pad. He looked up in sudden alarm and said, "Hey—you don't suppose that stuff could be any good, do you?"

"Beats me," Jensen said as he went to the door. "Seems a few people think so." He studied the worried expression on the wholesaler's face and decided not to say anything about the two bottles with the Ancient Vulture label on them. Kemp didn't look so good as it was.

CHAPTER 5

He found a parking space near the office and headed for the building.

Purvis was at his desk. As agent-in-charge, he had a chair which both rotated and tilted back. The other desks came with chairs which turned but did not tilt. Purvis turned and tilted and eyed Jensen, waiting.

"Well, they're pushing some of it here. Wholesalers are hurting but they haven't figured out why yet." He shed his hat and raincoat. "I'm trying to get a line on a couple of sellers tonight."

"Johnny called in. Sounded like he's having a ball. He's organizing an after-hours drinking bout in a parlor house."

"Guess he'll make it back in a couple of days." Jensen dropped into a chair, hiked it around until the wheels caught on a ridge in the floor and leaned back. He propped his feet on the desk and gave Purvis a detailed report, then asked, "Hear anything from the lab yet?"

"No. But I picked up quite a file from the attorney general's staff. They turned up quite a collection of characters a couple of years ago. You'll have to be Mighty Coyote around that bunch."

"I intend to be. Who's the tall dog?"

"Jim Wright."

Jensen whistled. "I thought he was dead by now."

"Know him?"

"No. I didn't know Costello either, but I heard about the guy and none of what I heard was good. Let's see … Wright … busy man twenty years ago. Gambling, southern Illinois, Capone alumnus, had a horse wire setup. That went sour and he turned up in Nevada, where they didn't like him either. I lose him there."

"He supposedly quit the rackets. The way they all do—get into something legitimate. He's ranching, has a lot of commercial property. The A.G.'s men twisted his tail good when they had the flap a couple of years ago. He came out clean, at least from a legal point of view. They couldn't even turn up enough to ask him any questions in front of the grand jury."

"He probably owned the grand jury anyhow," Jensen said sourly.

"He's not keeping many old-timers around. Dutchy Rohan's with him. Manages a roadhouse called the Gold Gulch Inn. Dutchy's about the same age. Hitting sixty. Started out driving a brewery team on the near North Side in Chi, got in with Jim and just hung on. Never did much to get his name in the papers. He never was a gun. For that matter, Wright wasn't either."

"Guns come cheap. How many square feet of the courthouse does he own?"

"This isn't as up to date as it could be," Purvis said, thumbing through the folder. "Probably one county supervisor. I made a wrong guess on that D.A. they kicked out. I thought he was Wright's lad but Robbie said he was on the other side. He got to raising hell about pinball machines. Wright evidently didn't own any but he does control a number of bars and other locations where the things were making him a good percentage. Evidently Wright set the kid up and got him booted for misconduct in office. Except they couldn't hang it on old Jim."

Jensen went to his desk, got a crusted, stubby pipe from a drawer, helped himself to Purvis' tobacco and fired it up. Cigarettes made him edgy; with a pipe going he could think better.

"The sheriff is a tame old toad named Tap Winters. He'll hang up his guns this year and there'll probably be a wild scramble for the job."

"But who'll get it?"

"You're a cynical lad." Purvis consulted another page. "If Winters stays in until election, it could be anybody. Word is that he'll retire this spring. If he'd recommend his undersheriff, a guy named Brud Cousins, the A.G. would be happy. Cousins is apparently all cop."

"So who will Winters recommend?"

"Maybe nobody. He needed Cousins when he stood for election because the guy is popular and efficient. He won't need him anymore. The board of supervisors would make an interim appointment. A stalwart and fearless citizen name Frank Lepage has said he wants the job. Lepage is a private dick, and quite an unusual one, Kon."

"You mean he walks around on a leash held by Wright?"

"I didn't say that. A few years ago he was doing the

heel-and-toe bit around Seacliff shaking doors. Didn't have a crying dime. Along came a young tiger named McCullough Shannon. Loaded with money, I guess. He went in with Lepage and they now have a sweet patrol business going. More men and cars than the sheriff, a new building, their own radio setup. And they apparently do one hell of a good job without stepping on toes."

"Maybe no toes have been in the way yet," Jensen retorted. "Sounds like a good squad."

"Sure. But they behave, and there's nothing to tie them to Wright. And nothing to show Wright isn't as good a citizen now as you or I."

"Oh, yeah."

"Well, we've got a few people going for us. Cousins, probably, if we need a cop we can trust. And Hank Murdoch is fixing Johnny up with a cover job."

"Who's Murdoch?"

"He served under me in the old O.S.S. in Europe. A good officer. He's editor of the *Seacliff Globe*. Johnny's a darned good photographer and he'll show up there to work in a week or so."

"What about me? What do I do?"

"You stay here temporarily, see what you can turn up in the city."

"Just one man on a deal like that?" Jensen protested.

Purvis ignored him and returned to the folder. "We have an ace down in the hole. A retired Treasury agent has been in Seacliff for some years. Oman Holbrook—know him?"

"No. Must have been before my time."

"Most of his service was on the East Coast."

"What's he do now?"

"Nothing much. Runs a little bar and keeps an ear to the ground."

"Then he must be a little deaf if there's a cooker operating in the county and he hasn't come up with a tip."

"Be intelligent about this, Kon," Purvis snapped. "The one place in the state where it must be utterly impossible to buy some of that hooch is in Rio de Oro County. And you can bet none of the stuff that goes into it comes from here."

"Suppose so," Jensen conceded. "I didn't mean to cast an aspersion on an old grad."

Purvis checked his watch. "Forget it. I didn't growl on purpose. What's your plan for the rest of the day?"

"Get a change of clothes and clean up. See if I can pick a up a lead on where they're pushing the stuff in town."

Purvis stood. His voice was serious as he said, "Don't take any long chances, Kon. We can afford to spend a lot of time on this one."

He finished shaving and showered and watched his refection in the big mirror on the bathroom door as he dried off. He was big-boned but there was enough muscle on his frame to keep him from looking rangy. His short, light hair lay close to his skull under the water. He considered his face and was satisfied with it.

He dressed carefully in white shirt, dark tie and suit and plain black shoes, and slipped a flat .380 Walther into the holster on his left hip after checking the clip. He took a dark gray snap-brim hat from the closet, set it on his head, got his topcoat and went out.

The rain had stopped and the solid clouds were breaking up into platoons that marched across the sky in front of a stiff northwesterly wind. He went to the bar and found Collie in a booth toward the rear. Her slim fingers played along the stem of a cocktail glass. The green eyes looked up at him and she moved over, said, "Sit down, quick. And get us a couple of drinks."

He slid into the booth, signaled the waitress. When she came he said, "Irish coffee and another of those bilious looking things Collie's drinking."

"Grasshopper," the girl said, and moved away. She was small, dark, and fragile-looking.

"What's wrong, Irish?" he asked.

"Results too quickly. I made the pitch about wanting to buy some liquor at the right price. A girl called Ginny said she'd see if she could help me out. I didn't know she meant right that minute."

"You mean they've been here and gone?" he asked in dismay.

"No. But I'm expecting someone any minute. Ginny made a phone call. Right after that there was one for me. A man said he heard I was in the market. He asked how many cases I'd want and what brands. I said that would depend on the price and we went on like that for a while. I tried to get a name or a number to call back but he wouldn't give me any. Finally he said he'd come in and talk to me if I'd wait a little while. I'm waiting."

"I don't like it," he said tersely. "This Ginny still here?"

"No. She left about half an hour ago."

"Alone?"

"Yes. Why?"

"Maybe nothing. Did she, by any chance, get a phone call first?"

"Let me think … yes. I'm quite sure she did."

"In a hurry?"

"She didn't seem to be. It may have been just another date. She's a regular here."

"Yeah. Look, I could be overcautious, but it sounds like they wanted to check back on you. This is almost like peddling dope. You don't sell to just anybody."

"What's bad about that? Why should I disturb them?"

"You go out with me. They could find that out, and also find out I'm a cop."

The dark girl brought their drinks. Jensen took a big swallow of his and glared at the glass.

"Do you think they'd try to do anything to me?"

"Possibly. More than likely they'd drop you fast and play it more cautious." Jensen was angry with himself. It had been a calculated risk; if they did check on Collie's friends and turned him up, there was a chance they'd make him for a federal agent. If that happened, the odds were long that the whole operation would shut down for an indefinite period. Unless the still kept running, his chance of finding it was about one in a thousand. And although his name and photo had never been in the newspapers, a limited number of people knew who he was. Most of these were higher-ups in the liquor industry, but the bootleggers certainly had their pipelines into such places. And into other police agencies, where officers involved in liquor raids had come in contact with him. Mentally he cursed his lack of judgement as he said, "Sit tight. I'll make a call."

He hurried to the phone booth at the back of the bar. With the glass door pulled shut he dropped a dime into the slot, thought a moment, then dialed Levine's number. Levine lived in an apartment building less than a mile away, and if he could just catch him at home …

He heard the buzzing on the line as the other phone rang. Then it stopped and he was talking before the other agent had finished saying hello.

"Sid—Jensen. Might have a tail job right now and I can't handle it myself." He told Levine the essentials.

"On the way, Squarehead. How do I know the guy?"

"Just come in the bar. The girl's in the second booth from the back. I may be there too …" He broke off as a man came in, spoke briefly to the bartender, then approached Collie. He saw him speak to her and remove his hat, then sit down. "He's here now, Sid. Dark blue suit, light blue shirt, five-seven, maybe one-forty, one-fifty at the most. Carrying a dark topcoat, wears a gray fedora. Swarthy face, prominent nose, wearing glasses with heavy rims. About forty. We'll hold him until you show."

"Five minutes." Levine hung up.

Jensen left the booth, knowing he was taking another calculated risk. There was a possibility the man in the booth would know him by sight, although he was a total stranger to Jensen. But the half-consumed glass of Irish coffee was on the table and the "salesman" would soon start to wonder where Collie's companion was and why he didn't show up. He approached the booth from the man's rear, caught Collie's eye and touched his finger to his lips.

"Hi. I guess you're the gentleman who called. I'm Jack Conrad." He slid into his seat and they shook hands across the table.

"I'm Mr. Welsh." The voice was mild and friendly but the dark eyes were penetrating behind the glasses. Jensen knew this was a man who would remember him if they met again. "It's a pleasure, Mr. Conrad."

"Hope we're not making you work overtime," Jensen said easily. "Have a drink?"

"No, I—well, I believe I will at that, thank you. Bourbon and soda, please."

Jensen called the waitress and gave the order. After she had brought it and left them, he said, "I hear you can make us a good deal on whisky. How good?"

Welsh sipped his drink. Without taking his eyes from Jensen's face he lowered the glass and said, "On some certain whiskies I'm sure we can. The domestic brands and perhaps a good Canadian. But no Scotch whisky, and we handle only a small amount of vodka. The price would depend upon the brand or brands you select, of course, and upon the size of the order. Ours is a large organization, sir, and we sell both wholesale and retail, although nothing smaller than a case."

"I like that wholesale route," Jensen said.

"There is a saving, although not as great as you might imagine. Do you have access to a liquor license?"

"You mean I've got to have a license to buy from you?"

"At a wholesale price, one is required."

"Well, I guess that kills that deal."

Jensen wondered if this was part of the standard pitch or whether "Welsh" had smelled a rat. He imagined the dapper man's name was nothing like Welsh. Now Welsh was puckering his lips and looking at Collie.

"Something might be arranged. If the young lady works in the cocktail lounge here, perhaps you could buy through their license."

"Good lord no!" Collie said quickly. "The manager barely tolerates the help drinking here."

"Too bad," Welsh said. "Still ..." He turned back to Jensen. "There are ways. How many cases did you have in mind?"

"There we talk price again, Mr. Welsh. I had ten or so in mind, if we can reorder later."

Welsh clucked his tongue. "I'm sorry. Such a small amount would have to be retail in any case. And frankly, I don't know how long our present supply will hold out. You might be able to reorder in a month and you might not."

"How's that?" Jensen thought of the story he had invented for Collie. He was interested to hear what Welsh's version would be.

"Because our price is so low. Sometimes we sell for less than your neighborhood liquor store has to pay for a brand. We can do that because we have no warehousing costs, no inventories in our own name and an extremely low overhead. We are in business courtesy of the federal government."

Jensen thought, *That's for sure, but not for long.* He sipped his drink and almost choked. "How's that?"

Welsh took his time lighting a cigarette. "A number of distillers were afraid, because of the unsettled world conditions in recent years, that there would be another world war. They remembered World War II and the great shortage of liquor. To avoid such a thing again, they made tremendous amounts of whisky, much of it under bond.

"The government crossed them up recently by ruling that the federal tax, in excess of ten dollars a gallon, must be paid when the whisky reached its bonded age. This whether it was sold or not. In at least one case, more than a million gallons is involved. What happens when that distiller has to put up better than ten million dollars in taxes on liquor he may not sell for five or six years?" He sipped his drink.

"I get the picture. Just the interest would eat up whatever profit there was in the stuff," Jensen agreed. He decided it was not too bad a yarn. Such a proposal had been made, but it had been defeated; which no one in the market for cheap hooch would bother checking.

"Exactly," Welsh went on. "Our organization was formed with sufficient capital to buy huge quantities of this fine whisky. Instead of making say, a dollar on a quart, the distiller makes twelve cents. But he makes it instead of losing it. Our deliveries are direct from the distillery."

"I see," Jensen said. He concluded even the best of lies has a touch of the truth in it; he conceded that deliveries were direct from the distillery. "Tell you what, Mr. Welsh. I belong to a couple of clubs which have liquor licenses." He looked in the back-bar mirror and saw Levine, in topcoat and hat, nursing a beer near the door. "Suppose I check with the stewards and see if they aren't interested. I could buy on those licenses and probably take a truckload. If the price is right."

"Fine, fine. Here—I shouldn't do this, but I will because I'm sure we're going to do business." He drew a printed sheet of paper from the slim briefcase beside him, scratched out figures and wrote others in their place with a ballpoint pen. "Here. This is a list of the brands we have in stock at the moment. I've scratched out the retail charges and put down the wholesale rate. And if you should manage to take a truckload, you can discount the total five per cent. We'll bill you for the entire amount and you can take the five as commission."

Jensen studied the sheet, controlling an urge to grab the man opposite him by the neck and talk longer with him in a certain basement room in the Federal Building. "That's a good deal. Thirty days on this?"

"Sorry," Welsh said with a bland smile. "We're too new a firm to carry accounts even that long. Deliveries are COD. If we had to keep an accounting department, we couldn't make prices like these."

"Sure. I suppose we can manage one way or another." Jensen folded the sheet and slipped it into his pocket. "It'll take a couple of days. Where's your office, Mr. Welsh?"

"I don't have one in the city because I'm on the road most of the time. In fact I'm leaving tonight for San Diego." He took a card from a thin leather case and wrote on it. "I have an answering service. You can call me at this number and I'll contact you as soon as I return, Mr. Conrad."

"Good. Have another drink?"

Welsh looked at his watch. "Thank you, but no. I'm late as it is."

They exchanged goodbyes. Jensen stood as Welsh left the booth and saw that Levine was gone from his stool. H knew the other agent would be waiting outside to pick Welsh up as he left the bar. He sat down again.

"Another?" he asked Collie.

She shook her head. "Not now. Not here. If you'll take me to my place I'll feed you."

"It's not too late to eat out."

"No. After sitting here trying to look doe-eyed and dumb for half an hour while you two told lies to each other, I want to be someplace where I can put my head back and laugh like a hyena."

"I'm for that."

"Then let's go. Buy a bottle on the way. Make sure whatever it is isn't on that list in your pocket."

CHAPTER 6

He built Scotch highballs in squat glasses which held a lot more than they appeared to hold, and swallowed a straight shot while she carved slabs of white meat from a turkey and made sandwiches.

"Turkey sandwiches and Scotch," she said. "Ugh."

"Scotch is good for you."

They ate without conversation. Jensen listened to the throbbing music and thought about Welsh. After a minute of that he decided it had been a long enough day and there would be plenty of time to consider Welsh after Levine reported in in the morning. He disposed of four sandwiches, loosened his belt and muttered, "What any girl living alone wants with a brute of a bird like that I don't know."

"Maybe to feed all her many friends."

"Bah!" He reached for a cigarette. "Isn't it time for you to say 'Just a minute while I get into something a little more comfortable,' Irish? I'll build new drinks while you do."

She shifted against him. He turned her head up and kissed her, met both cooperation and control. "I'm comfortable like this. Really. But I will go peel the nylons off. They slow the blood circulation in my beautiful legs."

"By all means. Do it now." He topped up the drinks and brought the bottle and a bowl of ice from the refrigerator. He checked the lock on the hall door, took off his jacket, dropped the Walther into one of the pockets and tossed it over a chair. He opened his collar, loosened his tie, kicked the shoes off his feet and stretched out on the sofa. Then Collie came out and he said: "Well, you did that much, anyway."

"You expected more?"

"I knew better." He caught her hand, pulled her down beside him and kissed her again. Then she drew back.

"Kon … what about Welsh?"

"Forget Welsh. I have."

"No! I want to talk a little." She twisted in his arms, grabbed the nearest glass, put it to his mouth. "Drink."

He sipped it, watching her eyes. They were huge and dark in the faint light from the teevee lamp and the fireplace.

She took it from him and drained it. He caught the top of her blouse, flipped it open and kissed her throat. She caught her breath and moaned softly and whispered, "I'm afraid …"

"Of Welsh?" he muttered. His fingers found another button, peeled the cloth back. He kissed her shoulder. "Don't be. A little man followed him when he left."

Her fingers dug into his hair. "I don't mean Welsh. I'm afraid of us …"

Later, in the big bed that was warm and scented by their bodies, she cried. There was no sound but he could feel the dampness of tears on her face and the shaking of her body. Still later, as he drowsed with the deep red hair brushing his face, she kissed him and drew him to her again.

He smoked a final cigarette and watched the sleek ivory form as she put their clothes on hangers and turned out the light in the living room.

Jensen phoned in at eight o'clock, hoping there was no reason to go to the office. He thought of how much better he would feel with a couple of hours more sleep, then gave it up. Collie looked as good in the morning as she did at night. Matty said Leonard Purvis, Johnny Levangie and Sid Levine were awaiting the honor of his presence so he would please get the hell down to the mine. He sighed, hung up, went to the bedroom and kissed Collie.

"This isn't going to be a regular thing," she told him.

"I didn't say a word."

She laughed lightly. "Whatever you get, you'll earn."

"Piece work," he said, and ducked as she rolled over in bed and hurled an ashtray at him. It shattered against the door as he went through.

The city lay bright and clear in the sun. Whipped-cream clouds hung in the sky and the bay was a clean, white-capped blue. He drove quickly to the office.

The others looked up expectantly when he came in. He gave Purvis the price list and poured a cup of black coffee for himself, then reported on the conversation with Welsh.

"The bastard foxed us," Levine said. "He got on the

plane all right, ticketed through to San Diego. I had men waiting there and in L.A. but he piled off at San Jose. Which we didn't discover until the plane got to L.A. And besides which we didn't have anybody to send to San Jose."

"San Jose is the closest airline stop to Seacliff," Purvis. "It fits. We'll have Jensen set up a small buy in a few days and see what happens then."

"So we get a delivery boy," Levangie said glumly. He had been up all night and looked it.

"Probably not that much," Jensen said. "Know what'll happen? The stuff will get here by Railway Express or some private truck line. COD, with no way to trace the shipper."

"We have to try it anyway," Purvis said. He turned to Levangie. "Pack your gear and report to Murdoch at the *Globe* in Seacliff. You don't look in shape to stand another night in the city."

"Yeah." Levangie yawned and stood, stretching. "You called it, dad." He waved and went out.

"Kon, better let things coast here until you make contact with Mr. Welsh again. Get hold of the Coast and geodetic survey maps of the country down there and get an idea of what it looks like."

"You sending us both after all?" Jensen asked hopefully.

"Not yet. First I want you to know that county like your own home. Every bit of water, every building that could possibly be involved. It's all on the maps." Purvis poured coffee for himself. "Now—there's a helicopter outfit down at Fort Ord, which is not too far from Seacliff. I pulled a couple of strings and they're going to practice low-level training flights over the country we're interested in. You'll go along to see what you can see. There'll be aerial photos taken at five hundred feet above the terrain. In color. Also infrared films will be made. We can be sure this plant is well hidden, but its heat may give it away. Got it?"

"Yessir. I'll drive down to Ord this morning."

"No. They'll have a liaison plane at International Airport for you in an hour. Be there."

He drove to his apartment for the traveling bag which was always packed, locked his car in the basement garage and called Collie. The phone rang half a dozen times before she answered.

"I've got to go out of town a few days. Maybe two or three."

"Did you wake me up just to tell me *that?*" She sounded sleepy and irritable.

"Yeah," he retorted. "I thought you might like to know. Sorry!"

He heard soft laughter. "You're sweet. Take care."

"Sure." He hung up and phoned for a cab. He rode it to Union Square, where he caught the airport limousine.

The helicopter pilots were good. In three days they took Jensen over Rio de Oro County literally foot-by-foot, flapping down box canyons walled by primitive mountains heavily forested by redwoods, riding turbulent wind currents, frightening half-wild cattle on the lower hills where the trees gave way to broad expanses of range grass. They followed fast rivers and lazy streams to their headwaters while he looked for signs of pollution. Nights, in a darkened room at the fort, Jensen studied the color slides taken by the aerial photographers, comparing them with the government maps, searching for uncharted structures. His head ached intolerably from the prolonged viewing and when it was over he had no more idea of where the operation was then he'd started with. There were no signs of activity in the wrong places, no tell-tale columns of smoke to finger the cooker. He brought a packing box full of color transparencies back to San Francisco with him.

He reported by phone to Purvis, went directly to his apartment and slept twenty hours. On the following day he left a message with Welsh's answering service. Welsh called on the third day and Jensen ordered thirty cases of liquor delivered to the steward of an athletic and social club.

When the liquor arrived it was brought by a commercial trucker. Tracing the waybill led to a dead-end in Fresno, some two hundred miles farther from San Francisco than Seacliff.

"You called it the first night, Kon," Purvis said testily. "The sons must haul it in two or three directions before they send it where it's headed. We can't put men on every loading dock in the state."

"Yeah," Jensen agreed. He inspected the shipment. There were five nationally-advertised brands involved. Each was an excellent counterfeit.

"At least people won't be going blind on the stuff," Purvis said. "The lab says it's all good, could probably do all right on the market if whoever makes it wanted to go legit. It's even aged a little."

"Darned little, I'll bet," Jensen said.

"At least a year."

"Like they planned to stay in business a good long time. But it's still hard to take. Why would a 'shiner hold onto it a minute longer than he had to?"

Purvis shrugged. "Maybe it took a long time to set up this distribution system. Or they could figure they're well enough hidden to run for years."

"I hope that's it," Jensen said softly. "Lord, how I hope the bastards get a little too smug."

"We want them all, Kon. Not just the still and a couple of guys. Something like this needs big people."

"We'll get the big people," Jensen promised.

It dragged.

Jensen prowled the streets of San Francisco as the days built into weeks. He drank in South-of-the-Slot gin mills, consumed a lot of bad but legal whisky, listening. There were no leads. He drank in after-hours bottle clubs which were raided without result by agents of the state's Alcohol Beverage Control Board. Periodic shakedowns of cabbies, news vendors and bellhops who could come up with a bottle for a price turned up a few specimens. The little guys who were caught in the net talked but had nothing to say. They took agents to rundown buildings where they had bought pints by the case. The locations changed from day to day.

Jensen learned nothing except that the bootleg was being bottled in various sizes.

He wrangled invitations to upper-crust parties and the result was the same, except that the stuff was going in quarts and case lots.

He became irritable. He saw Collie Fitzgerald a few times. Twice he fell asleep on the big sofa and awoke hours later, finding himself alone, with a blanket drawn over him.

It was four-thirty in the morning, after he had been on the case more than a month, when the persistent ringing of the phone in his apartment woke him.

"Kon—are you awake?" He recognized Purvis' voice.

"I am now." He yawned and reached for a cigarette from the nightstand.

"I just had a call from Captain Searle."

"Huh?" He found a match, got the cigarette going. "Who?"

"The Highway Patrol officer. Wake up!"

"Yeah," Jensen mumbled. "Yeah. Go on."

"Somebody shot Johnny a couple of hours ago."

"Oh, Christ!" Jensen reached for his clothes. He was completely awake now. "Oh, Christ."

"They shot him in the back, Kon. They killed him."

CHAPTER 7

They assembled in the office at dawn. A small group of quiet men with the mark of interrupted sleep on their faces. Gray faces, unshaven, angry.

Levine was there, tieless, his sparse hair uncombed. Murthy and Snyder and Musgrave were there, drinking coffee that was hot and black and bitter in their mouths. Jensen stared out the window at the borning day, hands thrust hard the pockets of his topcoat.

It was bad enough for the others, he thought. They knew Johnny, they liked him, they had depended on him sometimes in the past for their lives, and he had depended on them. But he had been Jensen's partner.

The others understood this and left him alone.

Purvis had a ravished look on his long, bony face, and Jensen knew what the old man was feeling.

With rigid control, Purvis drew himself up at the head of the long table.

"We don't know much yet," he said quietly. "We'd know nothing at all except that Captain Searle knew who Lev was and got in touch with me as soon as he heard. He said Johnny was shot in the act of cracking a safe at the Gold Gulch Inn."

"Which just happens to be owned by one Jim Wright," Jensen said bitterly.

"Yes. Gentlemen, how do we handle it?" Purvis said.

"This is no time to get a rational answer for a question like that," Jensen retorted. "Who did it? Did Searle say?"

"McCullough Shannon."

"A goddamned door shaker!" Jensen said bitterly. He glared at the men around the table. "Looks like Johnny got hot on something so they set him up."

"I imagine that's what it was," Purvis said quietly. "Again, how do we handle it?"

"With enough men," Musgrave said tentatively, "we could hit that place. Check every damned building in the county if we had to. We'd find it."

"We want more than a building with a piece of machinery," Purvis said. "We want people. We want them so we can take them into court and convict them."

"Of murder," Jensen said. His eyes were a dead, cold gray now.

"I know," Musgrave said. "I wasn't suggesting it."

"They must be sure of themselves, killing an agent," Jensen said.

"Perhaps they didn't know he was," Purvis said. "It may be they just figured him for a nosy newspaperman."

"Yeah. Guys who are smart enough to set up a pot like this one and run it at least a year aren't stupid enough to buy federal heat," Musgrave said.

"I want them. Personally," Jensen said.

Purvis rubbed his jaw. "I anticipated that. How do you propose to go about getting them?"

"I don't know. I've still got those private investigator credentials. No cover's going to be worth much, anyway."

"Perhaps," Purvis replied after a moment. "They wouldn't expect a federal man to come in as a private."

"They may not expect a federal at all," Jensen said.

"What's your story? You'll need one."

"Hell, I don't know. Just say his family doesn't believe the damn thing, wants to clear his name. Some crap."

"Johnny doesn't have a family, Kon," Purvis said.

"Then we'll invent one, damn it."

"All right." Purvis refilled his cup. "You'll have to wait a day or two."

"Yeah. It'll look okay then," Jensen growled. "And we'll see what kind of whitewash they give this Shannon."

"I think it might be good to have at least one more man in the scene," Purvis mused.

"Nuts!" Jensen rubbed the beard stubble on his face. "Just one thing. Searle knows who I am. Let's not have any others knowing it. That goes for old war buddies and retired T-men." He saw the fire rising in Purvis' eyes and hurried on. "I don't know that your friends Murdoch and Holbrook let anything slip. I just don't want to give anybody a chance at my neck."

He picked up his hat and went out.

Jensen drove the coupe without urgency. He passed sawmills and abandoned mining sites before the redwoods thinned and the slopes became less sharp, giving way to gently-rolling land where white-faced cattle grazed. He gave particular attention to Jim Wright's ranch. It was well enclosed by barbed-wire fences in good condition. Halfway up a hill to his right he could see the red-painted pens of a large feed lot where cattle were fattened for market. A spur track from the railroad that went on up the valley to the logging camps angled past the feed lot to a group of buildings that looked like storehouses. The main ranch house, a rambling, white-stucco structure in the Monterey style, was not visible from the road.

Seacliff was primarily a tourist town, with more than its normal quota of motels and restaurants and bars and an amusement park on the beach and a long, shaggy finger of wharf sticking out into the bay.

Jensen drove slowly, wishing Levangie had put more of what he found out on paper. Johnny had had a photographic memory and, unless pressed by higher authority, seldom filed a report until he was ready to close a case.

He found the motel where Levangie had stayed. It amounted to a score of cottages overlooking the tidal river which split Seacliff in two ragged parts. The man behind the counter was middle-aged. Sunburned scalp showed on the top of his head and he wore loose-fitting denim jacket and slacks. He put aside a newspaper and stood, rubbing his belly on the edge of the counter, as Jensen came in. He nodded and flipped a registration card over.

"Hi. Be here a couple of days?"

Jensen used a pen that was chained down. "More likely a week. That okay?"

"Sure thing. But steelhead season's on now and the town's full of fishermen. Got to charge a daily rate."

"Okay." Jensen replaced the pen. "I'd like number 9 if it's available."

He watched the man's eyes. Johnny Levangie had used that unit. "Sure. But it's a single. Nothing classy."

"That's okay. I'm traveling alone."

The man sucked his pendulous lower lip and his eyes wet questioning behind rimless glasses. Jensen stared hard at him.

"I know the last party in number 9 was killed." He took a small leather case from his breast pocket, flipped it open, showed the man the small silver shield and the identification. "I'm looking into it, Mister ..."

"Adams," the man said quickly. "Ed Adams. I'm the manager here." He cleared his throat. "We got some bad publicity out of that thing. Lot of gawkers coming around, nobody signing in. I was hoping the cops were through with us. After all, the man was miles away when he got shot."

"I'm a private investigator. Just happen to be a friend of the family. His folks won't believe he was a burglar, Ed. I told them I'd look into it."

Ed Adams nodded sympathetically. "He did seem nice enough. Real interested in the country around here. We had a couple of beers and talked some. Course, you can never tell ..."

Adams shrugged, suggesting it was all beyond him.

He took a key from the board on the wall and came from behind the counter. His feet bulged in rope sandals and he moved as though his arches were fallen. Jensen followed him in a small cabin and waited while the door was unlocked. Adams performed the ritual of sliding a window halfway open, checking the glasses on the shelf in the bathroom and handing over the key. "Think you'll find anything here?"

Jensen peeled off his jacket and tossed it on the bed. He watched Adams' eyes narrow at the sight of his gun.

"Probably not. I suppose the police looked."

"Cops went through like the place had bugs, which it hasn't. If they found anything, they didn't tell me."

Jensen had expected as much. "Know who was in charge?"

"Brud Cousins, the undersheriff. A good man."

Jensen grunted. If the attorney general's report had been right, Cousins was a good officer. "How come the sheriff? This is in the city limits."

"The man was killed in the county. City cops don't borrow trouble here."

"Uh-huh. How about his stuff?"

"I got it locked up. Cousins went through his gear."

"I'll want to do the same."

Adams lingered in the doorway. "Well—I guess it'll be okay. Now I don't like to bring this up, but there's eight days rent due. I don't own the place, just manage, you under—"

"I understand," Jensen said curtly. "Add it to my

bill."

"Surely. Thank you." Adams shut the door.

Jensen studied the room carefully. It was typical for a motel of this sort. A large bed, Hollywood style, with headboard. A bureau to match, with mirror. A luggage rack, small writing table with wastebasket and stationery. A phone on the table and a floor lamp beside it. A thin but durable carpet was on the floor and there were two occasional chairs. The room had one large closet and the bathroom had the usual fixtures. Jensen went out, drove the hardtop into the carport beside the unit and brought his single suitcase in. He took his time changing into faded denim slacks, loafers and sports shirt.

He set about searching the cabin.

He had no idea of what he might find, if anything. He knew only that Johnny Levangie wouldn't have used any of the usual hiding places. He ignored the bed, did not bother yanking the bureau drawers to look at their undersides. He assumed Cousins would have checked all these and more anyway.

Half an hour later, Jensen gave up. He went back to the motel office, found Adams manipulating cords at the small switchboard. Adams depressed a key, put the phone down.

"You turn it upside down on me again?"

"It wasn't necessary. I'd like to see his gear now."

"Out in the storeroom. Come on."

Adams led him to a windowless room illuminated by two naked light bulbs in ceiling fixtures, pointed to some suitcases, cardboard suitcases and clothing on a rack. "There it is. In that corner. Rest of the stuff belongs to other folks. People leave the damnedest things behind them."

That's right, Jensen thought. The damnedest things. Like their lives, sometimes. He asked, "That all of it?"

"All but the cameras. I didn't want to leave anything as valuable as them in here. The cops took all the film and I got the cameras in the safe out front." Adams squatted, pulled a long, slender paper-wrapped package from a low shelf. "There's this stuff too. Sporting goods store delivered it the evening he got killed. Poor guy never had a chance to unwrap it. And that's all. Pull the door shut when you finish. It'll lock by itself."

Jensen went through the suitcases and cartons carefully, without finding anything that appeared significant. There was a lightweight portable typewriter but no paper. He checked the clothes without result, not expecting to find anything now. Johnny had known the ropes; he was not one to leave something which could get him in trouble lying around. If he had put anything on paper, the chances were he had photographed it and burned the original, exposing the film so that anyone attempting to develop it in the normal fashion would destroy the latent images.

Since the police had taken the film, Jensen assumed they had already processed it and drawn a series of blanks. He frowned and unwrapped the package from the sports shop. It held a trout rod, spinning reel, line, leaders, assortment of flies and hooks and a jar of salmon roe.

He whistled softly. Johnny Levangie was no fisherman. If he bought fishing tackle, it was business, not pleasure.

Fish live in water. Water is the one essential in the making of whisky or any other beverage.

The fishing gear told Jensen that Johnny had either found or knew where to look for the water source. It told him a mountain stream was involved, one which the big, silver-sided steelhead would go up to spawn. One where there would be no reason to suspect the presence of an angler. It was the thinnest of leads.

CHAPTER 8

He found Adams still in the office. The manager leaned its stomach on the counter, rubbed it back and forth and asked, "Do any good?"

"Probably not. How about the cameras?"

"Right here." Adams swung the door of an old safe open and brought out three cameras. They were a Speed Graph with flashgun, a Rollei and a Leica with a lens that looked like a locomotive headlight.

Jensen inspected them quickly, unscrewed the base of the flashgun, found nothing but batteries inside. "This is all there was?"

"All I found."

"He must have had a gadget bag."

"Huh?"

"Big leather bag for film and flashbulbs and stuff."

"I didn't see it. Might be in his car. That's impounded."

"Okay. Thanks." Jensen went to his room long enough to strap his gun on and get a jacket. He backed the coupe from the carport, got a pair of sunglasses from the dash compartment and put them on. He drove down Pacific Avenue toward the civic center with a black Pontiac sedan showing in the rearview mirror. It had a tall radio antenna and had been parked at the curb near the motel.

He parked near the courthouse, got out and took his

time feeding the parking meter. The Pontiac rolled by and the driver angled into a parking slot. Jensen leaned against the meter post and watched the man climb out and approach him.

A big man, a little over six feet tall, and chunky. He moved in a way that said he might have been hot stuff on a college gridiron fifteen or twenty years earlier. His features were heavy but not unpleasant and his eyes were steady as he stopped with a few feet separating them. Jensen knew he was being studied, committed to memory. The big man produced a leather case with a gold star and ID card.

"Brud Cousins. Undersheriff." The voice was soft. "Would you come with me, please."

"All right. I suppose you know who I am, but take a look anyway." Jensen produced his credentials that said he was a private detective. Cousins read them thoroughly, until the waiting became uncomfortable. Jensen said, "I haven't had a chance to eat. How about lunch and a beer while we talk?"

What might have been a smile flickered on Cousins' face. He returned the case and said, "I wasn't going to take you to the office. Too many ears there, Jensen."

They walked together to the corner, to an Italian cafe. It was close to the courthouse, city hall and the police station. The bar was of dark, carved wood and the wall behind it was covered with mounted hunting trophies. There were booths on their right and a small kitchen at the far end where a fat man with long white hair sweated over a range.

Jensen turned toward a booth but the big man took his elbow and steered him toward a stairway leading to an upper floor. The odors of roast beef and baked ham were heavy in the cafe. They passed a gleaming coffee urn and espresso machine and Cousins waved to a thin, swarthy bartender. They went up the stairs and Cousins unlocked a door to a small private dining room, stood aside for Jensen to enter. There was a huge, round table circled by captain's chairs. The table and chairs were scratched and needed painting.

Cousins waved toward a chair and said, "Shirttail relations of mine run the joint. It's not bugged."

"I can talk for the record," Jensen said. He dropped into a chair, propped a knee on the edge of the table and began stuffing his pipe.

An aproned man came in, lugging a small bucket of ice. It held four bottles of beer. He uncapped two and set the bucket on the table and said, "You guys wanta eat?"

"Yeah." Cousins rubbed a bottle with his big hand. "The roast beef smelled okay. How about some glasses."

"You never use glasses." The waiter shut the door.

Jensen drank. The beer was fresh and cold in his throat. He smiled and said, "Old man Adams didn't waste any time calling you."

"Private men are expected to make a courtesy call on the sheriff here."

"I was on my way."

"After you'd searched Levangie's stuff."

"It was handy. Am I in trouble?"

"Not yet," Cousins replied slowly. "What's your angle?"

Jensen told him his story. Cousins' eyes gave no indication of whether it was being accepted. The undersheriff got a cigarette going, drank more beer and began peeling the label from the bottle. "That all of it?"

"Sure."

"You say you knew this Levangie. That you can buy him doing a little breaking and entering to get a story but not for stealing."

"I don't know any details. That's a first impression." Jensen sucked at his pipe. "I understand that Gold Gulch Inn is owned by Jim Wright. I imagine there's still a story or two left in the old bugger."

"That box he was working on had close to twenty grand in it, friend. He had the dial half knocked off when Shannon got to him."

"If you say so." Jensen stared at the big man. "Shannon a friend of yours?"

Cousins snorted. "If he is I don't need enemies. I ran him through the wringer but what in hell can you do when he sits there and says, 'Sure, I shot the guy. Caught him with the meat in his mouth and he made a break.' I looked pretty hard. I'm willing to look some more. But so far the story stands up."

"Uh-huh. I hear Shannon draws quite a bit of water."

"Not yet he doesn't," Cousins snapped.

The waiter brought the food; big plates of rare roast beef and mashed potatoes and vegetables and bowls of thin, clear soup. They began to eat. Jensen buttered a chunk of crisp Italian bread and said, "But he might if your boss quits. Yes?"

"Word does get around," Cousins said wearily. "Yeah. Tap Winters is going to quit in a few weeks. I want the job, but he's not about to recommend me. I doubt he'll come out publicly and say Frank Lepage should have it. But he's an old pedro-playing buddy of the board of supervisors. That's enough."

"Small-town politics," Jensen agreed. "How about if Lepage gets in. Is that bad?"

Cousins speared a chunk of beef. "You tell me. I think Wright's backing him in this Coast Patrol Service. But so far he and Shannon have taken a lot of pains to run it straight. This thing with Levangie is the first rough deal to come along." He chewed a moment, swallowed. "Maybe it's personal with me. I work hard at my job. Someday I want the big white hat. Along come these two characters with connections enough to euchre me out. So I don't like them much at all."

"Maybe I'll get lucky and turn up something so this blows up in their faces."

"Understand something, Jensen. What I feel personally about those two or anyone else doesn't count. My job is to see the sheriff's office is run right. As long as I carry the star, I'll do it. Operate inside the law and I'm for you. Step outside it and you're up the creek."

"That's fine," Jensen said. He wondered if Cousins had copy of his oath framed in the office.

"Don't forget it." Cousins uncapped another beer. "Now I'll tell you something. Levangie doesn't check out."

"No?" Jensen wondered if this stubborn cop would dig far enough to uncover Levangie's real purpose.

"Too many blanks. Levangie was supposed to be a real hot newspaperman. But a floater. I checked back on the references he gave Hank Murdoch over at the *Globe* and know what? None of them ever heard of him. But Murdoch said he was competent and from what I saw of his work he was." Cousins sopped up the last of the gravy with a hunk of bread, popped it into his mouth, chewed and got a cigarette out. "So— who in hell was Johnny Levangie? What the hell was he up to?"

"As far as I knew he was a camera bum."

"Know something else, Jensen? We haven't even been able to find a next-of-kin. Haven't heard a word, and there been time for them to read the papers. Now you show up and tell old Adams at the motel you represent the family"

"That's the way it is."

"I won't ask you any more yet, fella," Cousins said softly. "Know why? Because I think there's something pretty damned big in the air. I'm curious enough to want to see what it is."

"I've told you all I can. Can I ask a question?"

"Go ahead."

"Adams said you picked up some film. I'd like to see what was on it. Also a copy of your official report."

"The films were all blank. Our darkroom man must have goofed." Cousins leaned back in his chair. "The press has read the report. You might as well too. Drop by the office later."

"Will do." They stood and Jensen put money on the table. He was not at all happy with the interview. Cousins had served notice that he knew something was up and would be watching. And that he would not stand still for any jackassing around with the law.

They went down the stairs and Jensen thought he had learned at least one fact. Whatever Levangie had been up to, he wasn't trying to get into that safe when he was killed. Cousins had said the dial was half knocked off.

And Jensen knew Levangie had been capable of opening anything less than a bank vault with nothing but his sensitive fingers.

They stood on the sidewalk in front of the building, watching the noontime exodus of people from offices.

"One more thing," Jensen said. "How about the girl Levangie was with earlier?"

Cousins stuck his fists in his pockets and scowled. "I wondered when you'd get to her. She's okay. Rhody Cranston, reporter on the *Globe*. Big, leggy blonde with a nice face and nicer body. Smart girl. In her early twenties. She has the courthouse beat, which includes our office. Writes a fair story, isn't about to go for too many lies. She's been around a couple of years and lives alone. I understand she's got some family, but I don't know where."

"Ummmmm." Jensen relit his pipe. "Was she something big with Levangie?"

Cousins chuckled. "That girl could be something big with me, and I've got a wife that checks in at 36-24-36 after three kids. She's something big with Shannon."

"Yeah. Levangie takes the bimbo out. Afterwards, he gets killed by Shannon."

Cousins laughed. "Too pat. And it doesn't fit Shannon. He does all right. I don't think it would have entered his head that anyone could take a woman he wanted."

"One of those, huh?" Jensen stared angrily at his hands. "This Shannon still walking around with a gun?"

"Coroner's jury called it justifiable homicide yesterday."

Jensen said a four-letter word. He turned on his heel and went to look for Rhody Cranston.

The *Globe* building was a block off Pacific Avenue; a two-story structure of tinted concrete block, pink granite facade and lots of glass. Jensen went to the reception desk in the lobby, learned the city room deadline was almost an hour away. He went to the library on the second floor. The librarian was an old man with the look of a pastured-out reporter. He squinted over his glasses at Jensen's identification.

"Cop, eh?" The pale lips made a thin chuckle. "Son, I haven't got a parking tag since I sold the Essex. Course, I was police reporter then and could have got it fixed anyhow. So I guess you don't want me. What's on your mind?"

"I'd like to look through your clip files, Mister …"

"Sheerin," the old man said. "Harold Sheerin. Now I could help circulation along by tellin' you to buy the sheet instead of readin' it free. But I won't. Which ones you want?"

"Whatever you've got on Cully Shannon. His boss and the outfit he works for. I'll start with them."

Harold Sheerin leaned forward and asked, "You looking into Johnny Levangie gettin' killed?"

Jensen nodded.

"Good. I liked that boy. When he came up here, he wasn't too big to pass the time of day with an old museum piece like me … which most of these young pups won't."

He shuffled off and returned several minutes later with a fistful of bulging envelopes. He pushed them at Jensen and said, "Funny. Kids around this place always in a hurry. They'll come up and ruin their eyes on that old print or the microfilm machine for hours when they most of the time could ask me what they want to know about the old days and find out the easy way. I'm seventy-five. Born here and lived here all my life. Now, maybe I can save you a little time."

Jensen grinned. "Until I get some background, I won't know what questions to ask. I'll yell then."

"You do that."

Jensen settled himself in a wooden chair at a large table and began to read. There was little that hadn't been covered in the attorney general's investigation, but there was a picture of McCullough Shannon.

It showed a tall, lean man with a hawkish profile, strong jaw and wideset eyes that were compelling even in the photograph. He wore a uniform similar to that of the Highway Patrol, except that his hat was broad-brimmed.

In the printed account of the killing, Shannon claimed he had been making a routine check of the Gold Gulch Inn when he had seen a flicker of light inside. He had called on the radio for help and entered the building with a passkey. Caught at the safe, Levangie had attempted to escape, had kept running after a warning shot was fired into the ceiling. The second bullet had brought him down.

A deputy sheriff who had been nearby arrived at that point. He had heard the shots and confirmed Shannon's story.

Angrily, Jensen shoved the clips into the envelopes as the presses in the basement began their run. He went down to the newsroom. It was a typical layout for a small-city daily. To the right of the entrance was a glass-walled cubicle labeled, *Managing Editor.* Desks of reporters and rewrite men were banked side-by-side in two rows. The city desk was on a dais at the far end of the room, beside the horseshoe copy desk with its pneumatic tubes to the composing room.

Most of the desks were vacant but the city editor and his assistant flipped quickly through the first copies of the afternoon edition. A huge man was hunched over a desk in the managing editor's office.

Jensen opened the door and went in, saw the shaggy head raise. The face looked as though it had been chiseled from a redwood log. Black eyes regarded Jensen in annoyance.

"Yes?" The word had a quarterdeck ring to it.

Jensen said nothing for a moment. He studied Hank Murdoch, thinking, *this is one man who knew Johnny's real job. Leonard Purvis trusts him. He looks solid, but I trust nobody; a man without secrets cannot betray them.*

Jensen showed his identification. "I want to know about Johnny Levangie."

"Drag up a chair," Murdoch said curtly. He did not offer to shake hands. "Private cop … who sent you?"

"A client." Jensen filled his pipe. "A client who doesn't believe something's true just because it's printed."

"What we like. A doubting reader." Murdoch rocked back in his chair, took his time lighting a cigar. "This client wouldn't be Brud Cousins, would it?"

"I've met the undersheriff. Seems smart enough to make his own investigations."

"He also needs a red herring. He can't openly take his boss on. Not yet." Murdoch shrugged. "Forget it. It was just a guess. Maybe wishful thinking."

"You like Cousins."

"Let's just say I don't like anybody else."

"Okay. Let's talk about Levangie. What had he done to make him eligible for killing."

Murdoch blew smoke through his nostrils. "Beats me. I'll tell you this—he wasn't gumshoeing for me, but it puts the *Globe* in a rough spot. We've got to wash our hands of him publicly. Tell you something though. Maybe I shouldn't but I will. It was out-and-out murder."

"How so?"

"I can't go into it. Something might break later, but for now you can save your questions. Meanwhile, if you can turn up anything to break Shannon's story, I'm for you."

"Okay. What about the girl?"

"Rhody? Good kid." He leaned across the desk, stuck his head through the door and whistled softly through teeth. A girl at one of the desks raised her head, nodded. She walked toward them with easy, limber steps. Jensen could see how Johnny Levangie might have gone big for her.

She was tall, almost too tall for a girl. Fair skinned and slender, with high, prominent breasts, narrow waist and mobile hips. Her eyes and her tailored suit were the same shade of gray. There was a slight puffiness around her eyes, as though she might have cried recently. Murdoch introduced them and Jensen said he wanted to talk with her.

She looked at her wristwatch. "All right. I was just going to lunch."

"We can talk while you eat."

He walked her to the same cafe, to the same upstairs room. She ordered a steak sandwich and ate it without any sign of enthusiasm. It was a mechanical rite. Jensen nursed a beer until she was finished, wondering how well she had known Johnny. He sensed that this girl was normally a vibrant, happy creature. Today she was a manikin. He waited until she was drinking coffee before beginning the questions.

"Except for the man who killed him, you were the last person to see Johnny Levangie alive," he said. "I want to know everything he did that night. Everything he said."

She put her hands to her face and cried.

CHAPTER 9

He waited until she had herself under control.

"What good will it do?" she asked.

"I don't know. Maybe no good at all."

"I want to know something, Mr. Jensen," she said hesitantly. "Are you just a private detective?"

"Why do you ask?" Jensen said warily. "Does it matter?"

She refilled her coffee cup from the small pot on the table. "Simply because it seems rather soon for someone to bring an investigator in. And I'm quite sure Johnny was more than a photographer."

"How do you mean?"

"I had the impression Johnny was looking for someone. Or something. And you haven't answered my question."

"He was a friend. I know his family. His folks don't think he was a burglar. Neither do I."

"Oh." He thought she was going to cry again, but she swallowed audibly and went on. "I didn't know he had a family. If he *was* looking for someone, they must have known."

"His wife doesn't know. His kids are too young to know."

"Oh, God …" she murmured. "I went out with him. Several times. I thought he was single."

"They were separated." He held a match for her

cigarette. "Tell me about that night."

Her fingers toyed with a strand of wheat-blonde hair. "All right. But there's not much to tell. We'd both worked a little late at the paper. He asked me out and I said all right. We went to the Gold Gulch Inn."

"His selection or yours?" Jensen interjected.

"I—I guess it was mutual. It was foggy and damp in Seacliff and clear in the Valley. And at this time of year the Inn is about the only dinner house open up there. Anyway, we ate and there was nothing out of the ordinary. We had some drinks and we danced a few times. We left early, a little after ten."

"How about meeting people there?"

She ran her tongue over her upper lip. "There was a fair crowd. A few stopped at the table for a couple of minutes."

"You're a newspaper reporter. Which ones would you say were interesting?"

She got a cigarette from her purse and he held a match. Thoughtfully, she said, "In the light of what happened later, only a couple. Jim Wright, and Frank Lepage."

"Together?"

"Separately. But I remember seeing them at the bar together later." She puffed on the cigarette nervously. "It might mean nothing. What they said was just run-of-the-bar conversation, and Wright does own the place. Except for saying hello, Lepage talked just to me, sounding me out on what the *Globe* thinks about him."

"You don't recall *anything* significant?"

"No. Of course, I wasn't expecting—"

"Sure. Then you left. Why?"

"*Why?*" She mashed her cigarette out. "Because we just felt like moving on. We'd had enough of one place. We bar-hopped for an hour or so."

"And did nothing else?"

"All *right!*" she said fiercely. "We parked. We even necked a little. God, what an inquisition!"

"Don't go into orbit," Jensen said calmly. "I don't think Johnny had planned to go back there. I'm guessing but I think he saw or heard something that night. Later I'll probably ask you to take me over the whole route."

She looked him knowingly, scornfully. "I'm sure."

"Don't high-grade yourself, lady," he retorted.

She caught her breath. After a moment the red, sullen mouth smiled. "Sorry, Jensen. I suppose that sounded bitchy. But I'm blonde and I've got a body and men try for it."

"I understand. Didn't mean to burk." He swallowed some beer. "Okay. You bar-hopped. Meet any more interesting souls?"

She shook her head. "Most of the places were dead. In one or two we were the only customers. We worked our way down the valley toward town."

"Uh-huh. And he took you home without incident?"

"Not home. We were in my car; his was at the *Globe*. I said good night to him there."

"And you had no idea of where he was going?"

"No idea at all. He said something about home." She looked at her watch. "My lunch hour's about over."

"Well, thanks for talking with me." Jensen picked up the check. "If you don't mind putting up with more of me, I'd like to go over that route later. Can I take you to dinner?"

"I wouldn't be much company."

"I think you're fine company. What time?"

She managed a smile. "You'd never find my place. If you want to meet me after work at five you can follow me out."

"Good enough. I'll have plenty to do until then."

He left her on the sidewalk, watched the movement of her hips with appreciation as she walked along the street, a big, sleek girl with the sun in her hair.

Jensen looked up the sporting goods shop where Levangie had bought the fishing tackle. It was on Pacific, a few blocks from the *Globe*; a small store jammed with merchandise. A middle-aged man in a checkered shirt was arranging a display of lures in a showcase. He looked up and said, "G'd afternoon. Help you?"

Jensen showed his credentials. "You probably heard about the man getting shot the other night. I'm investigating."

The shopkeeper swallowed. His fingers made little smudges on the polished glass. "I read about it. Didn't know him, mister."

"No?" Jensen said sharply. "The day he died he

bought a trout rod, reel, line and other gear. You delivered them to his motel. But he was already dead then."

"Oh, golly! That the fellow?" Graying eyebrows shot up. "Sure, I remember him. Won't do much good, though. He just came in off the street, bought the stuff and left. Just like any other customer."

"He happen to say where he was going to fish? Or ask about conditions?"

"Nope. Most folks do but he didn't. I guessed he wouldn't do much good no matter what stream he hit."

"How come?"

A shrug. "It was plain to see he didn't know much about steelhead. Picked his gear like a kid buys candy. You know—gimme one a them an' one a those—just not right for this country. I fish 'em all and there's too much brush on the banks for that rod he bought. Should have been shorter. Line too heavy for the rod, too. Like he didn't care whether he never caught a fish. I tried to tell him about a few spots but I don't believe he paid attention. Not at all."

"He didn't pick up a map?"

"Nope. No map."

Jensen thanked him and left the phone number of the motel in case the man should remember anything else. He walked over to the sheriff's office and asked the deputy at the outer desk for Brud Cousins. The undersheriff appeared at the door of a small office and motioned him in.

"Doing any good?"

"Not so it shows." Jensen dropped into a chair beside the cluttered desk. "How about that report?"

Cousins was in shirtsleeves. He burrowed through the clutter, came up with a folder jammed with sheets of paper. There was an envelope stuffed with photographs taken on the scene. Jensen looked at the pictures and cursed softly. One showed Johnny Levangie lying face down on the floor. There was a small, dark spot on the back of his sports jacket. From the picture it appeared he had bled very little. There was another photo taken on a white table at the morgue. Jensen became sick with anger.

He read through the reports filled out by the first deputy on the scene, the captain of inspectors, the evidence technician, the autopsy surgeon. He studied a diagram of the building and the statement given by McCullough Shannon.

"Looks open and shut, doesn't it?" Cousins said when he had finished.

Jensen said a short, explosive word. He hurled the papers onto the desk and said, "I want Shannon charged with murder!"

"That's nice. I'd even like to oblige you," Cousins said mildly. "Just show me how to make it stick."

Jensen drummed his fingers on the desk. "A smart officer could make a case on this. It's full of holes."

"That a smart lawyer could plug. I know what you're thinking—the time element and the blood."

"So explain them," Jensen persisted. "The autopsy

says the type of wound wouldn't have caused death in less than five minutes, that it probably took ten. From the pictures, there wasn't much blood. If the man bled that long, he should have been lying in a lake of it. But your man said he heard the shots and Levangie was dead when he got to him within thirty seconds."

Cousins hooked his boot heels over the rungs of his chair. "Start with the deputy. A rookie—he never saw a man who'd just been shot before. He says he couldn't find a pulse. I'd guess that was because he was shaking too bad. Now, the bullet passed between the ribs, close to the spine, missing the heart. It severed an artery and there was heavy internal bleeding. They found more than a quart of blood in the stomach cavity. The bullet mushroomed against the breastbone and broke up into four pieces. The man fell face down. The only hole was in his back. What blood was still being pumped went into the stomach."

"If you say so," Jensen agreed reluctantly. "How about your man—is he on the take?"

"I doubt it," Cousins replied. "I doubt very many of them are. But they know Lepage is likely to be their next boss. The officer wouldn't falsify a report to save Shannon, but on the other hand I suppose he's human enough not to want his name on the firing list if Lepage gets it."

"Uh-huh. How about the slug?"

"Like I said, it broke up. Shannon carries a .44 Magnum."

"Which should punch a big hole going in and a bigger one coming out."

"Yeah. Except he wasn't carrying Magnum loads. I checked and his cartridges have a low muzzle velocity, less than that of a standard .38 service revolver."

"Uh-huh," Jensen said, unconvinced. He studied the scaled-off floor plan of the Inn. "You dig the warning shot out of the ceiling?"

Cousins shook his head. "Didn't seem to be much need to. Be a lot of trouble. There's a latticework thing hung from the ceiling in the hallway outside the office, with a mess of vines climbing through it. We found where the bullet went through the wood into the space between the ceiling and the roof. To get it out we'd have to chop a hole, and even then we might not find it."

"Digging a grave is a hell of a lot of work too," Jensen said tartly.

"Look—the deputy heard the shots. We got a slug out of Levangie. We know where the second one went."

"Well—I'm glad you're satisfied." Jensen stood and shoved his chair back. "How about a look at his possessions?"

"Okay. Come on down to the evidence room."

They went along a hallway to a windowless room lined a with steel lockers. Cousins unlocked one and emptied its contents on a table.

The fury built inside him again as Jensen inspected the bloodstained houndstooth tweed jacket, the white shirt. Levangie's gadget bag was there too. He checked it carefully. Mentally he inventoried the equipment.

"Where's the camera?" he asked Cousins.

"That's all we found."

"He have it with him?"

"No. It was locked up in the back of his car."

"Hmmmmm …" Jensen dug his pipe from a pocket and began to fill it. "Know something?" he said finally. "Here you have a newspaper photog. Their cameras are part of them, just like their heads. Levangie had three at the motel. He had the gadget bag in his car. But he didn't have a camera. Seem strange?"

Cousins chewed his lip. "I wondered a little about that myself. Thought maybe it was stolen or something. But I talked to the Cranston girl and she said she didn't see any camera. He carried the bag and she assumed there was one in it. I asked around at the paper and so far as anyone knew he only owned the three we found."

"I don't like it."

"It's a loose end. He could have had the camera in his car and dropped it off at his motel before he went back up the valley," Cousins said. "We don't know for sure that he went back to the motel, though."

Jensen sucked on his pipe. "Okay. Thanks a lot. I'll see you around."

He left the building, stood in the sun for a minute while he organized his thoughts and then he decided to call on McCullough Shannon.

CHAPTER 10

The building was low, sleekly modern with its facade of natural-finish redwood and canted glass. The outer lobby was furnished with a half-dozen chairs and a low table. To the right was a counter, behind which a crisply-uniformed man pecked at a typewriter on a stand near a shortwave radio console. Jensen decided the layout had cost somebody a lot of money.

"Hello. Help you?" The man came up to the counter.

"I want to see Shannon."

The man looked toward an inner door. "It might be a while. He's in with the boss now."

"Fine. I'll have words with both of them." Jensen went around the end of the counter, headed for the door.

"Hey! You can't—"

Jensen stopped with his hand on the knob. He met the man's eyes and said, "Sure I can."

He shoved against the door, found it locked. He banged on the smooth wood with his fist. The other man was saying something on an intercom box. Jensen heard a sharp reply, and the door was opened suddenly.

His stomach felt as though a big fist had closed on it. He stared hard at the man who had killed Johnny Levangie.

Shannon was tall, slender, with a thin face and hot,

dark eyes. His brown hair was parted on the left side and carefully combed. The fingers of his right hand hung close to the carved butt of a big revolver.

The slim automatic on Jensen's hip abruptly seemed inadequate. He stared at the dark eyes and said, "Do I come in or am I supposed to stand here until I get sick of the sight of you?"

Shannon's mouth became a slash, bracketed by little white lines of anger at the corners.

"Who the hell is it, Cully?" a man's voice called from inside the room.

"The guy who's been asking questions around," Shannon said. He moved aside. "Come on in, fellow."

Jensen found himself in an L-shaped room, a room designed to give comfort and impress. The walls were combed plywood in a natural shade. There was a big desk, and there was an expensive, high-backed swivel chair behind the desk.

A stocky, round-faced man sat in it, turning slowly from the window as they came in.

Jensen had a fast impression of pale, intelligent eyes, the beginning of jowls along the blocky jaw, of careful and thorough barbering of the steel-gray hair. Frank Lepage wore a dark business suit that minimized his bulk.

He rocked back in the chair, made a little tent of his fingers as he said, "I understand your name is Jensen and that you're a private investigator."

"I understand you murdered a man and plan to get away with it," Jensen retorted.

There was a crushing blow on the back of his neck. He felt his body go slack as nerve centers were scrambled. He stumbled forward into a red fog, felt the front of the desk bang against his legs. He sprawled across the smooth glass top, felt a sharp, crippling pain in his kidneys as he was hit from behind. He heard an agonized sound somewhere deep in his throat and he was being hoisted easily, spun around … Then Shannon was bending over him, yanking the Walther from its holster. Jensen cursed himself for a careless, cocky idiot.

Shannon hauled him from the floor and dumped him in a chair that was a deep, soft prison. Then the man was shaking him down with expert fingers, going through his wallet and ID case.

"What's it look like, Cully?" Lepage said.

"Like he's a private operator. We'll find out soon enough," Shannon said with a quiet certainty. He tossed the things in Jensen's lap. "Better talk, mister."

The pain was ebbing now, the muscle control returning. Jensen rubbed the back of his head, found a swelling but no break in the skin.

"About what?"

"You said something about a murder." Shannon's eyes mocked him. "From what I hear you've been a busy boy."

"I've talked to some people."

"Yeah. And all you've found out is that a burglar was shot in the act." Shannon sat on the edge of the desk and got a cigarette going. "If there was any more to it than that, Jensen, you wouldn't have to do any asking. Brud Cousins doesn't like me even a little bit." He blew smoke from his nose. "Let me tell you something. I didn't want to kill that man. I tried to wing him but he was moving fast and I got him for good. I'm not proud of it, but it happened. And the last thing we want here is a reputation for being trigger happy."

Jensen fingered his aching skull. "You proud of bending that cannon over my head from behind?"

Shannon's face darkened momentarily, then he grinned. "I got a short fuse, Jensen. I was about to go look you up anyway, after hearing how you put the heat on the Cranston girl. Then you walk in and pop off and I let you have it."

"Yeah, you sure did," Jensen said sourly.

Shannon picked up Jensen's gun, snapped the clip out, ejected the shell that was in the chamber and removed the shells in the clip. He dropped them into a wastebasket, rammed the empty clip into the gun and tossed it in Jensen's lap.

"Tell you something, private eye. If you've got a client, go earn your dough. But don't play it heavy. I happen to like that big blonde a lot, so don't raise your voice at all when you speak to her." He eyed the gun contemptuously. "And if you're smart, you'll toss that toy in the river. Try using it in this town and you could get hurt. Read me?"

Jensen rammed the gun into its holster. He picked himself out of the chair, feeling the sharp new pain in his kidneys. "I read you."

Lepage and Shannon were grinning as he walked out of the office.

Jensen went to his car and took his time reloading the .380. He stopped in a corner bar and had two straight shots and a bottle of beer. His head began to feel a little better.

He thought about Rhody Cranston. She had been dating Levangie. But McCullough Shannon had a proprietary feeling toward her. Jensen wondered just what its basis was. He looked at the clock on the wall and decided it was time to get cleaned up.

This would be no ordinary dinner date with a pretty girl. In the shower, he considered the possibilities and probabilities.

There was a possibility he would turn up some lead to whatever had made Johnny Levangie cut his date short and head back up the valley. Jensen considered it a thin one.

There was a probability that they would be followed by Cully Shannon or some of his door shakers. Shannon and Lepage would want to know every move he made from now on.

He tried to develop a theory on why Shannon had done what he had in the way he had. Jensen was reasonably sure Levangie had not been killed at the Gold Gulch Inn. He supposed the killing had taken place somewhere nearby and that Shannon had set up the scene, radioed a phony call for help and then fired his gun when he heard the deputy arrive.

But why?

Why there, when it meant bringing Jim Wright into the picture?

With miles of primitive country around, why not simply dump the body in a remote canyon?

He was still probing his mind for some reasonable thesis when he had finished dressing in his gray suit. He went to the *Globe* office, saw there was still some time before Rhody Cranston would be off shift and went upstairs to the library.

Harold Sheerin sat at an old desk, clipping stories from the day's paper and placing them in neat piles. He looked up, cracked a smile and said, "Hi, there. Think up any question for me yet?"

"Nothing specific." Jensen leaned on the desk. "But I was wondering what sort of things you and Johnny talked about when he came up."

"Just the old days. California, mostly."

"California what?"

"History," the old man snapped. He pointed to a large-scale map of the county. Jensen saw it was not a recent one; the paper was yellow with age. He read the legend and saw it had been drawn by a county engineer more than half a century ago.

"This was one of the first counties. We had a gold rush in the Fifties. Not like the Mother Lode, but enough so a couple of hundred shafts were sunk. Seacliff was the first place on the Coast between Los Angeles and San Francisco to get a railroad line to the interior valleys. That's what made it a resort town to start with. Old narrow-gauge. Used to take three engines to haul a train of logs over the hump," Sheerin went on. "All gone now, but I've got some old pictures of how it was in those days. Diamond-stack woodburning engines crawling up the valley. Not much of a railroad but it had the first tunnel in the north part of the state. Was a mountain in the way and they decided it would be easier to go through than around. None of it left now. Southern Pacific took over the line. They still go up in the logging country but there's nothing the same but the trees."

"Yeah. That's how it is everywhere," Jensen agreed. "That's all you and Johnny talked about? The old days?"

"Sometimes I think that's all I know anything about," Sheerin said. "We talked a lot but being a photographer; he was interested in the old pictures. Guess I got ten thousand of those out the house."

"Any particular type of picture?"

Sheerin sucked his cheeks in. "Can't say. I got them all catalogued. Couple of times he went through the index and got some out of the files."

"You wouldn't have any idea which ones?"

"Nope. Never happened to be watching. He wasn't making a list or anything."

Jensen sensed another defeat. Levangie had been an Easterner; he was no more interested in California history than in the sex life of an auk. But this ancient newspaperman had put him onto something—or his collection of old photos had. Fine. But what was it?

"Suppose I might get a look at this picture file of yours?"

Sheerin's bright eyes fastened on him. "You mean you think those old things had something to do with Johnny getting himself killed?"

"He could have seen something in one."

"Well, sure. I don't work tomorrow. Come on out." He wrote an address and gave it to Jensen. "Ten thousand pictures is a lot of pictures to look at."

"I know. But I'll have to do it."

The only thing he could hope for was that Levangie had made some kind of notations in the index. Knowing that Johnny seldom left a trace of his work behind him, Jensen doubted it. And anyway, what could a bunch of pictures that were probably half a century or more old have to do with the case.

The still certainly hadn't been running *that* long.

He went downstairs to meet Rhody Cranston. Hank Murdoch intercepted him at the newsroom door, beckoned him into his office and shut the door.

"Getting anywhere, Jensen?" The managing editor sat on the corner of his desk and rolled an unlighted cigar around in his mouth. His eyes searched Jensen's face relentlessly.

"Getting some people mad is about all."

"Uh-huh. Shannon was in. I saw him have a few words with Rhody and he went out of here like something scalded. Watch yourself."

"I plan to."

Murdoch got the cigar going. Thoughtfully he said,

"Still being just a private eye?"

"You saw my credentials," Jensen said shortly.

"I've seen mirages too," Murdoch retorted. "Okay. I won't push you."

"You said this morning Johnny was murdered. I know that. I knew it before I came down here. You hinted at his being more than a photographer. How about it?"

Murdoch chewed the cigar. Scowling, he said, "If your—*client*—is the person I have in mind, you know already. If it's someone else, you have no damn business knowing."

"Suit yourself." Jensen frowned but he was pleased. Murdoch knew what the word *security* meant. He had no doubt talked to Purvis on the phone by this time, and Purvis had apparently played it straight down the line.

"I'll take a little chance on you, though. If you get on a spot that's too hot, you can call me."

"Thanks. Good to know." Jensen left the office and went into the city room. Rhody Cranston saw him and left her desk.

"Want to stop for a drink first?" she asked. "We can miss rush hour traffic."

"Sure. Where?"

"I'll show you."

CHAPTER 11

It was called the Blind Pig, and set up along the classic speakeasy lines. Sawdust on the floor, murky lighting, a player piano banging away in a corner. A long bar without stools and a few old tables and chairs lined along the opposite side of the room. They went up one flight of stairs off an alley and Rhody used a key.

Jensen guessed there were fifty people inside. They were making enough noise for five hundred. Three of the ugliest bartenders he had ever seen worked in shirtsleeves. They squeezed up to the bar and Jensen heard a man complaining about his drink.

"If I could mix a drink I wouldn't be workin' in this jeezly hole," the bartender told him. He looked around, caught Rhody's eye and yelled, "Hi, cutie! What'll it be?"

"Something big and strong like you," she said, laughing.

The barman grinned and dumped ice into glasses. The man who had complained moved away and his place was taken by another.

"What kind of phony lash-up is this?" Jensen demanded.

"Don't say it so loud. You'll disillusion the trade."

The man beside him had spoken. Jensen saw he was tall, white-haired, with long arms and slender, delicate hands. He was watching Jensen with eyes that could have been either blue or gray, smiling easily.

"Kon, meet Oman Holbrook. He owns the place," Rhody said. "Oman, Kon Jensen."

They shook hands. Jensen found the man's fingers were like iron and his eyes searched the pale, smooth face for some sign of recognition. Holbrook, onetime T-man, had known who Johnny Levangie was.

"A pleasure, sir," Holbrook was saying, raising his voice to make himself heard above the racket. "I've been hearing about you."

"Already?" Jensen said.

Holbrook's bland face smiled. There were tall, iced glasses filled with pale liquid on the bar and Holbrook waved the bartender off. "I see a table in the corner."

When they were seated, Holbrook raised his glass. "To your mission, sir."

Jensen's face was expressionless. "What's that mean?"

Holbrook considered a thin line of bubbles rising in his glass. "I had met John Levangie. I was favorably impressed by him. Mister Shannon is not one of my favorite people. In fact, he is one of the few gentlemen in these parts who does not have a key to my door."

Jensen smiled. They drank, with Rhody watching both over her glass. Jensen almost choked.

"White lightning," he said wonderingly.

Holbrook chuckled. "We call it Mountain Meadows Mist. It comes in little stone jugs." He looked slowly over the crowded barroom and added, "They all drink it because I've made it fashionable. And not one in ten can stand the taste of the stuff."

"I'm the tenth one," Jensen said. "Take that lock off the door and you wouldn't have a dozen customers."

Holbrook nodded. "With a legal saloon on every corner, folks want something different. Adults who weren't even born in the Twenties read Fitzgerald and O'Hara and Thorne Smith today and wished they'd lived when the speaks were running. The Pig tries to give them the atmosphere of one."

"They were before my time, too."

"I knew them well," Holbrook replied. "I was a Prohi. Some of the agents I worked with are still with the Treasury Department. I see them once in a while."

Jensen smiled and said nothing. He finished his drink. Holbrook waved a hand and in a moment a fresh round was on the table.

"So what did you hear about me?" Jensen said suddenly.

"That you were stirring up a hornet's nest. That you paid a call on Shannon and Fatty Lepage and came away with a headache."

"Word does travel."

"This is a cop's hangout. And the chap who was minding the phone at Coast Patrol is with the bunch three tables down." Holbrook dug in a pocket and handed Jensen a brass key. "You might as well have one. Word will get back to McCullough Shannon and he'll dislike me even more. "

"Don't turn your back," Jensen said bitterly. He

finished his drink, checked his watch and told Rhody, "We better roll."

They said goodbye to Holbrook and went out. It was already dark, with the last streaks of sunset in the sky far over the ocean.

He followed her convertible through the north side of town and along a road that twisted into the foothill country. The house was small, with walls of post adobe and glass and a flat, sloping roof. It was remote, shaded by a white oak. The furnishings were modern and comfortable and there was a small bar built into the divider between the kitchen area and living room. He built a drink while she disappeared in another part of the house. He heard the sound of a shower and later the pad of bare feet on the tiled floor. When she came out she wore an unadorned black dress which hugged the curves and spike-heeled pumps. Her hair was up in a Grecian roll. Jensen caught his breath and handed her a drink. She thanked him with the soft gray eyes and sat on one of the leather-covered stools, crossed her legs.

"Nice, real nice, Rhody." His eyes moved from her, around the expensive room.

The pouting lips smiled. "If you mean the place, I don't do it on what the *Globe* pays. Daddy has a wad of oil wells."

"I like you better and better, girl." Jensen finished his drink. "Want to go in your car or mine?"

"Let's take mine. I've got a radio that picks up police calls." She gave him the keys and they left in the

Plymouth convertible. Rhody drew a fur cape over her shoulders and sat close to him.

The headlights picked out a Ford station wagon at a fork in the road. Jensen slowed, watched the rearview mirror. There were headlights a couple of hundred yards back. He made a couple of turns and the lights stayed with him. He pulled off the pavement where there was a wide shoulder.

"Want to get somebody unhappy?" he asked.

"What?" she said uncertainly.

The headlights were creeping up behind them now. He said, "That will be Mister Shannon."

She put a hand on his arm. "Jensen—I don't want any trouble. Just ignore him."

"He's a hard guy to ignore. Might as well get it over with." He put his arms around her and kissed her hard as the other car stopped about ten feet behind them. Her hands came up and cupped his head, drew him to her.

Jensen kept an eye open. When he heard the slam of a car door he twisted, pressing the girl back against the seat as his fingers worked the front of her dress open. He cupped the high, firm cone of her breast and felt her squirm against him, making little protesting sounds in her throat.

A flashlight beam speared through the window. Jensen ignored it.

There was a muttered curse and he heard the door handle click.

As the door opened he rolled away from the girl,

hurled himself out of the car. Shannon had his left hand on the door and the flashlight in his right. With the full momentum of his plunge behind him, Jensen drove the stiffened fingers of his right hand into Shannon's belly.

The tall man gurgled and reeled back. Jensen followed with a judo chop to the throat and Shannon tripped on his feet, fell on his back. The flashlight bounced on the hard ground and in its light Jensen could see Shannon's fingers groping for the butt of his service revolver. Jensen jumped and his heel landed on Shannon's wrist. There was a satisfying howl of pain. Jensen kicked the gun away as Shannon got to his knees. He waited a fraction of a second, hooked a right hand that found the hawk nose. He felt bone give way, saw a dark spurt of blood. With calm precision he drove the hard edge of his hand into a nerve center in Shannon's neck.

The big man lay still. He continued to bleed and he groaned and Jensen could see the buckshot eyes on him as he found the gun, dumped the shells out of it.

"I could kill you," Jensen said softly. "That's the state's job, but if you get out of line again I may do it anyway. Remember it, tough guy."

He tossed the gun down and turned back to the car. Rhody Cranston stood by the door, staring with immense eyes. Her dress was still unbuttoned and he could see the full curve of her breast. He took her arm and urged her into the Plymouth.

"Fix yourself up," he said quietly. "We'll go eat now."

She stared at him for a long time, not speaking. Then she closed her dress and turned on the car's interior light while she repaired her lipstick. She still had not spoken when Jensen parked in the lot beside the Gold Gulch Inn.

It was Monterey style, with whitewashed walls, a balconied upper floor and tile roof. It topped a knoll in a growth of pines and redwoods. There was a lane into the trees behind it and Jensen saw a cluster of cottages. There was a long, dim-lighted bar and lounge to the left of the main door. Hand-hewn posts supported immense ceiling beams and there was a small organ on a dais at the far end of the bar. Beyond, a stairway terminated at a heavy studded door. Jensen knew the room where Levangie had been killed was beyond that door.

The dining room was to the right. Rhody paused, said, "If you want to watch the people, we can eat in the bar."

"Fine." They found an empty, semi-circular booth. Jensen ordered martinis and steaks and lighted cigarettes for them. He said, "You look scared."

"I am," she said. "If I had any sense I'd leave right now and stay as far away from you as possible."

Jensen chuckled. "You saw how rough Shannon is."

"You don't know that man, Jensen," she said fiercely. "He won't let you get away with it."

"He killed one man this week," Jensen retorted. "He won't press his luck and try for two."

"He'll wait."

"He won't have time to wait. He's got a lot of people round here snowed. I say he's already running scared." The drinks came and he picked the olive from his, chewed it. "Level with me, Rhody. What is Shannon to you?"

She lowered her eyes. "Nothing. Except trouble, perhaps."

"That's now. What about before?"

"Before …?"

"Before he killed a man."

She took a deep breath, and her breasts came up full against the dress. "I used to go with him. Nothing steady or serious. He's a tiger, and some women need tigers. When it got to the point of being all claws, it ended."

"He warned me off you this afternoon."

"He never has admitted it's over." She drained her glass. "Do we have to talk about it?"

"Just one more thing. You were dating Johnny. Would Shannon have killed him otherwise?"

"Oh!" She shut her eyes tight. Finally she muttered, "I can't believe I had anything to do with it. I've gone with other men since. Cully's quick with his fists but … no. He wouldn't kill over any woman."

"I'll take your word for it. No more questions." He had felt they were pointless anyway, but wanted to eliminate any possibility of coincidence. A great many murders are committed because of women. "Here's dinner."

The steaks were thick and rare and tender, and

eating removed the need for finding a more pleasant line of conversation. They were finished and Jensen was ordering brandy and Benedictine when he saw Jim Wright and Dutchy Rohan coming.

Rohan was chubby, with a jowled moon of a face. Wright looked about as he had in the picture from the files; compact and trim, with the healthy look of a man who spent a lot of time outdoors and active. He wore a stockman's suit and pointed western boots. He and Rohan were making their way along the bar, stopping to talk with customers.

"Plug your ears." Jensen was lighting a cigarette. "The party could get rough."

Rohan started it, leaning on the end of the booth. "Dinner good, Rhody?"

She met Jensen's eyes before saying, "Fine, Dutchy. Hello, Jim. Counting the house?"

"Counting the people in it," Wright said. He smiled, watching Jensen, showing good teeth.

"Well, don't just stand there. Sit down and buy." Rhody slid around in the booth and introduced Jensen.

There was no pretense of shaking hands. "You're the private eye," Wright said. "Who's interested enough in a dead burglar to hire you?"

Jensen looked at him steadily, without expression.

"It bothers me to have something like that happen," Wright said. "But the officer was only doing a job."

"For you."

Wright's face darkened for an instant; then the smooth smile was back. "He was protecting my place of business."

"He's good at his work," Jensen said curtly. He flipped a business card across the table. "Better have your lawyer get in touch with me. The man's family might settle for the deed to this place and the liquor license. Fight it and we take your ranch and whatever else we can find!"

"So that's it. Shakedown." Wright lit a thin cigar. "Shamus, I don't shake. Go chase an ambulance before you need a ride in one."

"Whatever the rules are," Jensen said curtly. "Now, you two-bit hood, I bought a dinner in your clip joint and I wish you'd split out of here so I can digest it. Go on, scram."

Wright and Dutchy Rohan exchanged glances. Wright shrugged and they left. There was a man at the electric organ now, accompanied by a string bass and guitar. Jensen saw the nervous tension in Rhody's face and said, "Come on. Dance with me."

She started to rise, then said, "Would you mind if we had another drink first? I'm jumpy."

"Sure." Jensen signaled the cocktail waitress. Rhody reached for her cigarette pack, found it empty. She searched the large envelope purse she had brought.

"Want one of mine?" Jensen asked.

"Should be some here." Her mouth curled in exasperation and finally she tilted her purse, spilled the contents on the table. There was a pack of cigarettes in the pile. Jensen felt his usual awe at the volume and variety of items one woman could carry.

Mentally he began to count and classify them He saw a rectangular, silver-colored case and was instantly alert. He picked it up, pressed the catch. The flat lid opened and he saw it was half-full of cigarettes. It was a heavy affair, with a lighter built in.

"Nice piece of work."

"Why, that's not mine …" She looked at it a moment, and he saw shadows pass through her eyes. "I remember. Johnny had it the night we were here. I must have picked it up with the rest of my things when we left."

"I can return it to his wife. Might be better if she didn't get it from you."

"Yes—please."

Jensen slipped the case into his pocket. He knew why nobody had found a camera in Levangie's car. The cigarette case was the camera, a custom-built device for undercover work. Its concealed lens was smaller than the eraser on a pencil, but it could take sharp pictures under almost any light conditions.

He was also sure Rhody Cranston hadn't slipped it into her purse without realizing it. Johnny Levangie would never have left it lying on a table in a bar. No. He must have stumbled on something so hot it couldn't wait. He must have figured the odds and decided there was a good chance he wouldn't come back alive.

So he had left the camera someplace where he knew it would turn up. Slipped it into the girl's purse, knowing she'd find it within a few days. Knowing the men who came to finish his job would reach her.

His thoughts were broken up by the sight of three men bearing down on them. Brud Cousins, Hank Murdoch and a smaller, businessman type.

CHAPTER 12

Jensen met the businessman-type's eyes and changed the classification to cop-type. The balding, rotund man carried a large, metal-bound box of the type used to hold instruments.

Rhody caught his glance and whispered quickly, "Will Gorham, evidence technician."

Cousins was looking at the closed door to the second floor in a speculating way, as if he had ideas about finding a second bullet up there. Jensen wanted a look at the premises himself first.

"Gentlemen," Jensen said pleasantly as he slid from the booth. "Join us for a drink."

They sat down and he was introduced to Gorham. "Hear you think we only did half a job upstairs," Gorham said.

Jensen looked at the instrument case. "Well, you're back." The cocktail waitress came by and he told her to bring a round of drinks.

"Been here long enough to get into a beef?" Cousins asked.

Jensen made reproachful, clucking noises.

"Private Patrolman Shannon was just a customer at the Medical Center. Getting a tweaked beak repaired, among other things," Cousins said.

"Do tell." Jensen got a cigarette going. "Now how would the sheriff's office know something like that?"

"A deputy just happened to come upon Shannon watching a certain house."

"The deputy wouldn't just happen to have been there on purpose?" Jensen asked.

"Sheriff Winters would never permit something like that," Cousins said piously.

"Of course not." Jensen got up, said, "Back in a minute." He went to a short corridor leading to the rest rooms. There was a connecting door to the dining room. He went through it, stared down a wavy-haired headwaiter whose dark, bushy-browed eyes said catering to diners was not his first line of work, and found his way through the tables to a patio exit.

Outside, he could still hear music from the bar, and sounds from the kitchen. He stood in shadow, smoked half a cigarette, waiting for his eyes to adjust to the dark and to be sure he wasn't followed. Above was the balcony which circled the upper floor. He found a stairway and went up. Most of the windows were dark but there was pale light showing through the drawn curtains of one room. He remembered the floor plan from the sketch at the sheriff's office and concluded it was Dutchy Rohan's office. He put his ear to the glass but heard nothing. There was a heavy door with a lock that opened after a brief session with a pick.

Jensen used a pencil flashlight, found himself in an interior hallway. There were several doors. He recalled the floor plan again and eliminated most as leading to private dining rooms. The one he wanted was second on the right.

It was near this door that Levangie's body had been found. Hoping the original measurements had been somewhere near accurate, he estimated where Shannon had been standing when the shots were fired. He found a switch and the hallway brightened as lights concealed in the ceiling lattice came on. There were hammered copper planters spaced along the walls. Leafy vines grew from them to the latticework.

He probed the leaves with his flashlight, found the first bullet hole quickly. The slug had torn a chunk of wood from the lattice before plowing into the dark surface of the ceiling. He parted the leaves and studied the white ring of plaster around the hole.

Five minutes later he had found nothing more. The remainder of the ceiling was smooth, with a patina of dust which meant nobody had plastered over a second hole.

But the deputy sheriff had heard two shots. The second bullet had to be somewhere, unless Shannon had been telling the truth or had fired off one blank.

Jensen snorted and began going over the lattice itself inch-by-inch. The wooden grid swayed, thumped softly against the wall. He thought it was about to fall on his head, then saw it had been loosely suspended by sturdy hooks and eyes secured to the ceiling. Lifting an end released the pressure on the hooks there and they started to slide from the eyes.

Jensen lowered his arms, brushed dust from his hands and scowled at the contraption. It was then he saw one of the lamps among the leafy growth was not burning.

He peered at it, saw where the second slug had gone. The hole it punched in the lamp base showed only as a slightly darker spot. It looked like the bullet had gone in straight and torn the wiring loose. Jensen was up on his toes, pawing the branches away for a better look, when the stairway door opened.

He saw the wavy-haired headwaiter and a man in a mess jacket. He broke for the rear door and they came for him without a sound. They had guns but he didn't expect them to shoot with the cops downstairs. But they'd be on him before he would have time to get the heavy door open. If they didn't corner him in the narrow hallway, they'd have plenty of chance outside. He hit the unyielding door, spun round, braced himself to take them, wished he had more room to move. They were about a dozen feet away, with the headwaiter in the lead.

Jensen sprang from a crouch, caught the end of the lattice. His momentum drove it upward against the hooks and he felt them snap out of the eyes. With the weight of his body and a sharp tug he tore the wooden framework loose. It cracked sharply and the end slashed past his face like a huge axe. He saw the two heads pop up through separate leafy squares and the weight of the thing was bringing the two men down, pinning them to the floor. The hooks on the far end broke then. Jensen got the door open, ran along the balcony and down the stairway. He reentered the dining room, detoured into the rest room and scrubbed the grime from his hands.

There was too much noise in the bar to hear whatever racket the pair upstairs might be making. Jensen saw the stairway door was closed. He went to the table, sat beside Rhody and swallowed half his drink. He took money from his wallet and put it on the table.

"You got a Chessy cat look," Cousins said.

"This is an unsafe building," Jensen said, deadpan. "I was doing the tourist bit upstairs where they kill people and the roof fell down. Rather, the roof decoration fell down. I think it seriously injured a couple of citizens with guns who were standing under it."

"Just what the pure—" Cousins demanded.

"The ceiling had been weakened by a couple of bullet holes. One through the plaster and another in a light fixture."

"You leveling?"

"Well, they sure look like bullet holes."

"Come on, Will. Bring your stuff," Cousins ordered as he got up. "Murdoch, call the office and tell them I want a team of inspectors here *muy pronto*. Jensen, you stay right where you are!"

He hurried for the stairway with the evidence man following. There was a phone at the end of the bar. Hank Murdoch lumbered over to it. After a moment, Jensen followed.

"This thing is breaking too fast," he said when Murdoch hung up.

"You wanted to stick Shannon. Maybe you have."

Jensen studied the strong face, the shaggy head. He made his decision. "General Purvis said I could count on you. I don't like to count on anybody. But it looks like a long night and I've got something that's too hot to carry around. He took the disguised camera from his pocket, put it on the bar. "I don't know what's in this. But Johnny died to get it."

"I'll drive up tonight." He pocketed the camera.

"You know this is a top security project. Know where to go?"

Murdoch muttered a phone number.

"Okay. Better call. He'll probably want to meet you at the office."

"Any report?"

"Just tell him they're running. They don't know how much we haven't found out." He lit a cigarette. "One thing. They may decide it's time to really bounce me around. If they try, they'll get hurt and I may get in a jam. If I do, leave me there. I let Wright figure me for a shakedown artist. If nobody comes to help me it could convince him that's all I am."

"You got a lousy job. Good luck."

He returned to the table. "Looks like I either got to leave or answer a lot of questions."

"I'm ready. I'd like to know what happened up there."

"I'll need wheels, but you could hitch a ride home with the law. I think I'm hot."

"I'm with you."

"All right." They went from the bar out into the cool

of the night. Rhody was adjusting the fur cape as Jim Wright hurried up the steps. Jensen intercepted him. "Cousins is upstairs digging around for a couple of bullets."

Wright stiffened, growled, "What is this?"

"I found bullet holes. Plural. But Shannon said he only fired once at the ceiling."

"You nosey—"

Jensen laughed coldly. "Relax, pal. They'll only find one."

"Meaning?" Wright's voice was thin with fury.

"I got there first, dug out one slug. Just to see how hard you'll try to get it back, chumly." Before Wright could say more, Jensen was walking Rhody to the convertible. He headed up the valley.

"Are you bluffing, Kon. Or did you …"

"Yes and no. Show me a place we can watch the comings and goings and I'll fill you in."

She pointed out a narrow dirt road that twisted through the woods above the Inn. There was a small mesa grown over with range grass and sage. From the edge they could see the building, silver-white in the moon. Jensen lit cigarettes and told her what had happened.

She laughed at his version of the escape. They finished the cigarettes and Jensen shivered as a breeze came through the wind wing. She got a bottle of brandy from the glove compartment and they drank. He saw several cars leave the Gold Gulch Inn, and one with a tall antenna pulled up. She said the two men who got out were sheriff's inspectors.

He studied the delicate shading of the moonlight on her face. The brandy was hot in his stomach. He reached for her shoulders, turned her toward him and kissed her. It was better than it had been before, with headlights burning through the rear window. Her lips were hot and soft and sweet with lipstick. She twisted on the seat and her skirt slid up. Her thighs were sleek as silk.

Her mouth was on his ear and she was saying his name. "Mmmmm-m-m … button beside you … seat goes back more."

Jensen fumbled for the button with his left hand, found it. The seat bumped back and he slipped the Walther from its holster, dropped it on the floorboards. She was lying across the seat, eyes luminous as she reached to help him.

Somewhere in the valley a siren keened. Jensen froze, swore under his breath. It was moving fast. He sat up, reached for the gun.

Rhody Cranston screamed softly, deep in her throat. She curled into a ball on the seat, yanked her dress down on her legs with a vicious movement. She reached blindly for the brandy.

"Sorry as hell," he muttered. He lit two cigarettes, gave her one and nipped at the flask. The siren died out and he saw a coupe bounce into the parking lot, red spotlight flashing. Frank Lepage jumped out and hurried inside.

Now, if Lepage would just cooperate by getting

rattled and maybe make a run for the still to …

Too much to hope for, Jensen decided. Lepage was a front man. He would try to cover for Shannon. Jensen smoked his cigarette and did not look at the blonde girl. She seemed to have control of herself now.

"How long must we stay here?" she asked.

"I want to see where Lepage goes."

"It doesn't bother you a bit, does it."

"Of course it does," he snapped. "But there's nothing I can do about it so you might just as well stand at ease in the ranks. I'll make it up to you."

"You may not get a chance."

She did not speak again. A half hour passed before the coupe drove slowly away from the Inn. Jensen backed the convertible around and drove down the dirt road by moonlight. The coupe went by, heading up the valley fast, just before they reached the county road. Jensen gunned the Plymouth, drove without lights until a sharp bend put the other car out of sight.

Jensen hit the lights. The car was hurtling between jagged rocks on the left and the rim of a gorge on the right. He tried to think what this particular piece of land had looked like from the helicopter, remembered the drop was measured in hundreds of feet. The tail lights of the coupe were getting smaller, closer together. He shut the squeal of tires and the violent rocking of the light convertible from his mind and rode the gas hard. He knew where Lepage was headed—someplace on the Wright ranch. There was nothing else along this particular road, and the two gates were guarded. Unless he rode Lepage's bumper, the guards would probably riddle the car.

With Rhody along, he couldn't take a chance on that. He was easing off on the gas, ready to give it up, when he saw the flash of lights behind him.

The car was coming fast, driven by someone who knew just where he was going and the tricks of getting there.

"Get down!" he shouted. There was a wide, comparatively straight stretch ahead.

"*Why?*" She was watching the other car too.

Without taking his eyes from the road, he hit her just above her left ear. She slumped across him and he pushed her to the floor. The headlights were riding his bumper now.

He cut the wheel sharply to the right, straightened out and hit the brakes with both feet. There was a screech of metal against metal and the other car's bumper was raking the side of the Plymouth. He felt the right front wheel skid over the lip of the gorge.

He punched the gas, felt the rear wheels take hold. The car rocked violently, and then all four wheels were on solid ground. It banged into a deep spot where water had drained off and stopped. The impact drove him against the steering wheel, emptied his lungs as he grabbed for his gun.

There was an instant in which he saw the other car was a station wagon. It looked like the one Shannon drove. He had the Walther in his left hand then. There was no time to aim. He fired three times and then the wagon was going, digging out in a cloud of dust. Jensen leaned out the door and shot one more time, trying for the driver. The wagon veered to the left, scraped an outcropping of stone, straightened out and disappeared around a bend.

Jensen tried to breathe. There was sharp pain low in his chest and he guessed a rib had cracked. Rhody Cranston stirred. He dragged her onto the seat, leaned across her, got the door open. "Get out."

She stared at him and got out. He slammed the door, got the motor going again and trod on the gas. He supposed he had lost half a minute. The wagon had gone like something scalded and he thought there might be a mile between them before he got the Plymouth rolling as fast as the road would allow.

There was no sign of the station wagon when he reached the first ranch gate. If there was a guard, he wasn't in sight. Jensen spotlighted the dirt turnoff without picking up any tire marks. That left one more gate.

He found the fire about two hundred yards before he reached the gate. From the road it was only an orange light deep in the canyon, and there was a raw gap in the brush at the roadside. He parked and walked to the edge. By the light of the moon he could see a rock shelf ten or fifteen feet below. He made his way down and could see the flames, far below, spreading through the brush. The smell of smoke reached him and the heart of the fire burned fiercely, sent up a thick, dark column of smoke. He climbed back to the road and got a cigarette going.

There was no point to thinking further about Shannon. Nothing alive could have survived such a drop. If he had been thrown out on the way down, rescuers couldn't get to him until daylight anyway. He inspected the car. The left tail light was shattered. Both fenders and the door were battered. He got in, drove to the ranch gate and turned around. He could see the marks of one set of tires in the dirt. He went slowly down the grade until he found Rhody. She was walking, carrying her shoes. Her blonde hair had worked out of the roll and sprayed down her back. He stopped the car and she got in.

She took a cigarette from her purse, pushed the lighter in. "You didn't get him. What happened after you hit me?"

He told her. She whispered a single word. "Dead …"

"Probably. He tried to put us down there."

She swallowed audibly and found the brandy.

Brud Cousins was waiting at the Gold Gulch Inn, surrounded by plainclothesmen and a couple of uniformed deputies.

"Where the hell did you take off to?" he demanded. He bounced two flattened chunks of metal on the bar. "Here they are. I've put out word to pick Shannon up for a talk."

"You'll need a basket," Jensen said wearily. He reported what had happened.

"We'll let the Highway Patrol retrieve him." Cousins

made a phone call. He said, "They want for you to stick around. We'll need a formal statement too."

Jensen shrugged and settled down to wait.

They were big men, with hard, competent faces. Holstered guns slapped against their thighs as they walked in. Jensen explained what had happened. They inspected his driver's license and credentials.

"According to your story, you had trouble with Mister Shannon earlier. He came up behind you, tried to force you off the road. You fired a gun at him," the older of the two said.

"That's right. The undersheriff can fill you in on the case."

"We're concerned only with violations of the Motor Vehicle Code, sir. May I see your pistol?"

Jensen frowned. The patrolman didn't look like he wanted an argument. He handed the Walther to him.

"One shell under the hammer, two in the clip," the officer said. He read the serial number off and his partner wrote in a notebook. "Let's take a look at the car you were driving."

They went outside and inspected the Plymouth. Firmly but politely they invited Jensen to get in the rear seat of their cruiser. Rhody started to get in with him but the patrolmen shook their heads. They drove him to the scene. The fire had spread noticeably.

"Brush is too wet to burn much, but we'd better give Forestry a call," the driver said.

They left him in the car while they paced off skid marks on the pavement and made measurements.

They did the same at the point where the cars had sideswiped each other. One found a pair of empty shells ejected from the Walther. He put them in a white envelope and sealed it.

Jensen yawned. It was getting close to midnight. He said, "How about dropping me back at the Inn. I've got to see Cousins."

The one who had been making notes turned in the seat and shook his head. "We're taking you to the courthouse. There's a man from the D.A's. office on his way there now."

"And what for?" Jensen demanded.

"Mister, the best you can get out of this is a manslaughter charge, the way it sounds."

CHAPTER 13

Malcolm Tower had been waiting. So had a young deputy prosecutor. They had worked hard to break him. Jensen had wondered at first why they worked so hard until he remembered that Jim Wright had maneuvered the previous district attorney out of office. Presumably he had put the incumbent in.

Jensen knew there was not much they could do until they found a body. That wouldn't happen at least until daylight.

He was tired. He did not give a damn about anything except getting some sleep.

He did not even try to think about the case as the pills Bill Mayo had provided numbed the pain. He went to sleep with the overhead light shining in his eyes.

Morning was bad. His bones, muscles and internal organs either ached or were stiff. His head just ached. He woke when the kitchen trusty banged on the tank door with a ladle. He saw Mayo, still naked except for his shorts. go to the door and come back with two metal cups. They were filled with black, steaming coffee.

"Eye opener," Mayo said. "Lousy, but there's a lot of it. I told the runner to get us chow from the lunch wagon. Be here in a half hour or so."

Jensen rolled off the bunk, went to the sink and splashed water on his face. He tried the coffee. It was bad.

Mayo put on faded blue jeans, tennis shoes and a shirt. There were no other prisoners in the felony tank. The food came and they ate. It tasted like it had come from hash house.

"Hope they feed better in Quentin," Mayo grumbled.

"Murder second, huh?" Jensen said. Mayo did not look like a murderer to him. Mayo looked like a hell of a nice guy. "Rough jolt."

"Bum rap." Mayo flopped on the opposite bunk and blew smoke at the high ceiling. "I got lousy luck."

"Some of us do," Jensen said.

Brud Cousins came for him a few minutes after eight o'clock. They went to a small room on the same floor. It held nothing but a table and a couple of chairs. Cousins sat on the table and said, "Jensen, you fixed yourself up good."

"That's what the man said last night."

"Swasey got a brain concussion from that bit with the bench. You buggered up a good gun and broke Vance's pool cue when you tossed them out the window."

"Ask me why it happened," Jensen said curtly.

"I've got my ideas. Far as I'm concerned it never happened. But I want to know the truth of what went on up that road last night and just what you're really up to. This room isn't bugged, so we can talk."

Jensen lit a cigarette. "I'm still the private cop I was

yesterday. I told you how it was with Shannon."

"I might even believe you. The D.A. won't."

"Can't blame you much there. Find Shannon yet?"

"They're looking. It could take a long time. You want to be in here a long time?"

"Go talk to Rhody. She'll tell you how it was."

"I have. She remembers seeing lights. Then you hit her and the next thing she knew she was out of the car."

Jensen shrugged. "Guess I'll sit it out awhile."

"Suit yourself. I'm supposed to take you downstairs. Tower's ready for you again."

Tower did not give up until early afternoon. When they took him upstairs again, they said his lawyer was waiting. He met Sid Levine in the room where he had talked to Cousins.

"You could get in trouble, practicing law without a license," Jensen said.

"We can do time together. How's it going, Squarehead?"

"Not bad. I got some sleep, which is what I came here for."

"Purvis says he can spring you."

"Sure. But I've got Wright making me for a shakedown deal and the cops figure Shannon and I just locked horns over a woman. That won't go if I get out the easy way."

"Purvis said that too. He wonders if you can bust out of this can without getting killed."

"Maybe at night. Except when there's something doing, it looks like they just have one jailer who has to stay downstairs and run the radio."

"Try it. There's a parking lot on the back street. My car's there. You'll find clothes in the trunk. Also a Thompson gun and a pistol. Keys under the left rear fender skirt."

"You think of everything."

"We try."

"I took a chance on Murdoch last night. Gave him the trick camera of Johnny's."

"Purvis has it. When I left they hadn't finished with the film, so I don't know if he got anything we can use." Levine stood, slapped his hat on his head, shook hands. "Luck, Squarehead."

He went back to the felony tank. Bill Mayo talked him into a rubdown. It worked out as Jensen had expected. Instead of hurting in spots he ached all over. He was not taken down for more questioning. He spent the afternoon resting and listening to the small radio belonging to Mayo. He considered what he knew of the jail layout, seeking a possible means of escape. Several times he heard his name mentioned in news broadcasts. He was being held incommunicado. Shannon's uniform cap had been found over four hundred feet down the face of the mountain. It was now presumed his body had fallen all the way to the river and washed downstream.

He questioned Mayo at length about the jail routine. He discovered that when there wasn't too much noise, he could hear the patrol cars talking with the radio dispatcher on the floor below.

After supper, with about two hours to go until the reading lamps in the cells would be extinguished, Jensen said, "I would like to get out of this place."

"Sure. Just walk out." Mayo went back to a magazine.

"If you can figure a way to get the night jailer into the tank that's all it takes."

"He wouldn't come alone."

"He might if he thought one of us was dying and there weren't any deputies around."

Mayo put the magazine aside. "I can just about guarantee no deputies if you wait until the night patrols are all out. But he'd have a couple of big trusties along. Those mothers are worse than the fuzz, chum." He rubbed his jaw. "I got a heart condition and they feed me nitro pills when I need them. I can look pretty dead."

"We're in business." Jensen unplugged the small radio and ripped the cord loose from its terminals. He found a sharp end on a bunk spring and used it to separate the wires for a distance of about two feet. The tank door was hardened steel. He found a small gap in the edge strip and jammed one wire into it, several inches from the floor. He studied the marks made by the door as it rolled on its tracks, looped the free end of the wire around the frame with about two inches bare. He put the plug in its socket and lightly touched the loose end to the metal. There was a satisfying spark.

"How's it gonna work?" Mayo whispered.

"Like so. Jailer unlocks door, slides it back. One side of the wire is on the door. When it moves far enough, it makes contact with the other end. Should knock the man down, by which time we will be through the gate and all over whoever's standing around."

"I'm with you. If, as and when we're out, what happens then?"

"We're fugitives. The first cop to see us will probably shoot."

"Might as well be dead as the way I am."

They waited. Jensen listened carefully to the position reports of the night patrol cars at the nine o'clock time check. It sounded as though only two were on duty, with the nearest some twenty-five miles away.

"Buzz the man. I'll go into my act." Mayo lay on the cold floor, held his breath until his face reddened, then began to breathe in short, noisy gasps.

Jensen jammed his finger against a button on the wall. In a moment a voice on the intercom system demanded to know what was wrong.

"Mayo's having some kind of attack. He can't breathe," Jensen shouted. The voice said it would be right up.

Jensen plugged the cord in, checked the free end quickly and knelt on the floor, cradling Mayo's head. He heard the outer and inner doors open and close, and quick footsteps. It sounded like three men.

Through the grille, Jensen saw Vance and two tough

and solid-looking men in jail dungarees. He got up and started for the door.

"Okay, Jensen. Back off, away from the gate," Vance ordered. "I'm coming in and there's a couple of guys he to see you don't pull anything."

Jensen backed up against the nearest cell. It put him about eight feet from the door. He heard the lock open, watched the heavy door begin to move on its rollers. Bill Mayo rolled his head and made choking sounds. When the edge of the door was inches from the bare wire, Jenson hurled himself at it. As he moved, there was a crackle of sparks and he heard the jailer howl in surprise. He fell back against the nearest trusty.

Head lowered, Jensen plunged through the door. He slammed into Vance, drove a fist into the pit of his stomach. Vance howled again, doubled up and bounced off the wall. A trusty was swinging a wild right at his head. Jenson pivoted, caught the wrist, straightened. The man spun around him and his head slammed against the gate. Mayo was in it then and the third man was trying to run. Mayo grabbed, caught him by the top of his blue jeans. The tight pants came down around the trusty's knees. He was trying to pull them up when Mayo hit him behind the ear. Jensen grabbed the keys. Mayo tossed the three men into the tank and slammed the door. They went through the two outer doors as tumult broke loose in the other tanks.

They ran down the iron stairs to the second floor. Jensen started down the next flight but Mayo grabbed him. "No good that way. If a cruiser pulls in while you're in that courtyard you're a dead duck."

"Then how?" Jensen snapped.

"Out the front, just like we was people." Mayo yanked open a door leading to the sheriff's office proper. They were in the booking room.

"*Jensen!*"

He skidded to a stop, staring. Collie Fitzgerald was just getting up from the big bench. She wore a dark sweater and slacks and she looked tired.

"What're you doing here?" he demanded.

"I was trying to see you."

"Oh, God," Jensen muttered.

"Who's this?" Mayo said.

"A friend."

"I didn't think you had any. Gimme the keys and I'll grab our junk out of the property locker." Mayo took the jailer's keys and quickly opened a steel cabinet. He pawed through it, brought out two large envelopes, tossed one to Jensen. "Now let's get the hell out of here."

"Right," Jensen snapped. "See you, Irish."

They went through the front door of the sheriff's office fast, ran down the stairway to the street. There were no cars in sight when they reached the door. They walked to the corner at a normal pace.

"Well, guess we better split out, buddy," Mayo said. "If we're lucky we got fifteen minutes."

"I've got a car stashed."

"Better bust up. I got a friend in walking distance."

They shook hands quickly. Jensen crossed the street and walked rapidly toward the parking lot where Sid Levine had left the car. He heard running footsteps behind him. It was Collie Fitzgerald. He ran then, found the car. He was feeling for the keys under the fender skirt when she caught up with him.

"Collie—beat it before you get in trouble." He got the trunk open. In the light of an electrolier he could see a bundle of clothes. A stubby Police Special and box of shells were beside them. A Thompson gun, ammo drum in place, was on the floor. He slammed the trunk closed and unlocked the front of the car.

"Kon—where do you think you're going?"

Collie didn't show any intention of leaving. Jensen realized he had no idea of where to go until he could get organized. An alarm would certainly be out for him in half an hour, probably less. "I don't know, Irish."

"Breaking jail wasn't smart," she said. "But you can't sit here. My car is a block over. Drive by there and follow me. I've taken a motel for the night. It'll give you a chance to get organized."

"Don't be a fool. Don't get involved in this, Irish."

She got in beside him. "I'm both. Now drive."

He went past the sheriff's office. There was no visible activity as he let Collie out at her car. He followed as she drove across the river to a motel on the eastern edge of the city. It was a big place with only a few cars in the ports. They went in and he used the bath to change into clothes Levine had brought. When he finished dressing he found her sitting cross-legged on the bed. She had touched up her lipstick and she handed him a glass.

"Strong," he said, twisting his mouth at the taste. "You must have flipped, Irish."

"I only wanted to see you. Not help you break out of jail."

"So why did you?"

"Because I don't think you'd do what they say you did."

"I didn't."

She emptied her glass. "You haven't kissed me."

He kissed her. When it threatened to get out of hand he tore open the property envelope, retrieved his belt and shoelaces and wallet. He checked the contents, saw that his money was untouched. He found the slip of paper on which Harold Sheerin had written his phone number and address.

There was a phone booth outside the motel office. It was visible from the street but Jensen decided to chance it rather than use a house phone where the manager could listen in at the switchboard. He borrowed some dimes from Collie.

The phone rang a long time before the old newspaperman answered. Jensen identified himself and Sheerin said sharply, "How long you been out of jail?"

"Just a few minutes. Look, by any chance have you pinned down those old pictures Johnny was interested in?"

"Happens often. Not much of a jail." He heard

Sheerin chuckle. "Nope. Like I told you, there's thousands of 'em. I did remember one thing. Whatever got him going was something in that centennial edition we put out some months back. Get hold of a copy and you might see it yourself."

Jensen's hopes sank. He didn't think much of his chances. "Okay. First chance I get, I'll do that. Many thanks."

"Be careful, boy. You're not too popular."

Jensen hung up. He thought a moment, then looked up Hank Murdoch's number.

"You idiot. If you wanted out, we could have sprung you," Murdoch growled. "The night police reporter just called. You and the other guy are being looked for hard."

"I had to do it this way," Jensen said quickly. "Hank— I want to get into the *Globe* building and go through that centennial edition of yours."

"Damn! All right. I'll be there in fifteen minutes. Use the fire escape on the alley behind the building. I'll have the door unlocked."

He returned to the room, strapped the gun on his hip. Collie was combing her hair. "I've got to go."

She put the comb down, turned, drew him tight against her. She kissed him lightly and said, "Come back."

The alleyway was dark. Jensen ran lightly up the fire escape, pulled the door open. Murdoch waited, quickly slipped the bolt.

"Come on. I've got the thing down in the morgue."

The centennial edition ran to well over a hundred pages. Jensen stared at it and groaned.

"I'll help you," Murdoch said. "What do I look for?"

"First, if you've got the latest Coast and geodetic maps, dig out the ones that cover Wright's ranch. They should show all the roads and structures up there now." He paced the floor, got a cigarette going. "I've been all over them anyway and didn't turn up anything. But we need a water source and a site that's both concealable and accessible by truck. The still itself must be as big as a house, and it probably has a fifty-foot column. They've been keeping the juice a long time, and that means considerable storage space."

They began to read. Jensen started from the back of the paper. An hour later he was nearly halfway through and he had a headache. Murdoch grunted, jabbed a finger at an old picture.

"How about an old train wreck?"

"Let's look." Jensen eyed the picture. It showed a tiny locomotive and train of cars stacked up in a shallow canyon where a trestle had given way. It had happened sixty-one years before, and the engineer, fireman and head-end brakeman had been killed, according to the reproduction of the original account carried in the *Globe* of that time. Apparently the trestle footings had been undermined by a stream which flowed underground at that point. The train had been on a downgrade and had just left the tunnel which bored under the summit of the mountain range when the mishap occurred. The area was known as Gold Gulch and a number of deep-shaft mines had once been worked there. "This is it!"

"Except for one thing," Murdoch said. "That old tunnel fell in on itself years ago."

Jensen went over the government maps. There was no marking for the tunnel or even the old railroad. "They could have dug it out again, or enough to use. Whatever they did it's well buried because we couldn't spot it from the air. It could take days just to find where that old right-of-way went." He drummed his fingers on the table, stared glumly at the wall. He saw the old map hanging there. He checked the date. It had been drawn within five years of the wreck. With the excitement rising, he traced the old railroad line. The trestle and tunnel mouth showed.

Hurriedly he compared it with the government map. From the contour lines he estimated the portion of the tunnel on Wright's property ran from fifty to two hundred feet under the hill. A dirt road into the redwood logging area higher in the mountains passed close to it.

Jensen grabbed a telephone, told the operator to try Purvis at the bureau office and at home. In less than two minutes he was giving a terse account of what had happened and what he had found. He pinpointed the area from township lines on the map.

"We're rolling. You sit tight, Kon. It'll take us some time to round up enough men for the job. We'll take them early in the morning," Purvis said.

"Hold on," Jensen said urgently. "I could still be wrong. This is just an educated guess. The tunnel is a couple of miles in from the ranch headquarters and our birds could all be flying by the time we even found the way in. We've got to nail them on the scene or they'll weasel out."

"So?" Purvis sounded unhappy.

"I'll see what I can do about getting in there."

"Nonsense!" Purvis barked. "You're dead if they catch you. I order you not to attempt it!"

"We've both been behind enemy lines before, General." Jensen replied. "If they catch me, they might just take me where I want to go while they figure what to do about it."

He hung up on Purvis' protest. Hank Murdoch was watching him, shaking his head.

"You're asking for a pine box, Jensen."

"Johnny Levangie's already got one."

"Okay, you idiot bastard." He ground his cigar out on the floor. "Guess you could use some help."

"Thanks. But one man is harder to catch than two. I'm paid for this."

"Nuts!"

Jensen grinned. It was good to know a man was willing to go in with him. "You could do this. Get Captain Searle at the CHP. He knows who I am. If he can move a few men into the area they can sort of sit around and wait to see if a rumpus breaks out. He's not to tell any of them what's up until it starts."

Murdoch shrugged. "It's your show. When do you

want to roll?"

Jensen thought about it. The simplest way was often the most direct way. If he could get on the ranch about the time the day's work started, it might just be possible to find a likely prospect, stick a gun in his ribs and make the man take him where he wanted to go.

"Say about sunup. Searle can have the gates covered by then. I'll meet you at the fork in the road just below the Gold Gulch Inn. Got it?"

"Yeah. But I don't like it."

With the lights out, Jensen left the way he had come, and he reached the motel without passing a police cruiser.

CHAPTER 14

He woke before the alarm went off, showered, wished he had something to shave with. He was ready at quarter of six, with the eastern sky barely showing dawn. He went to the bed and shook Collie awake. She growled a protest and kicked at him.

"I'm going. Promise you won't come after me."

She sat up, shoved a pillow behind her back and reached for a cigarette. Jensen struck a match. She puffed and said, "Go away. I want to sleep. I came down to see how you were doing in jail and you took advantage of me."

Jensen laughed, mussed her hair and went out. The morning air was damp this close to the ocean. He went over his plan of action and finally admitted it wasn't worth much. What he needed was an easy way of getting through the gates of Jim Wright's ranch. On impulse, he went to the phone booth, found Rhody Cranston's number and dialed it.

She sounded wide awake as she said, "My God, the law has been here twice looking for you. Cousins is mad as a bat."

"Sure. You want in on something big?"

"You mean a story or just more of your trouble?"

"A story. There won't be any other reporters. It's big and it's all yours. I'll need a little help."

"If I helped you now I could never walk into a police

station again."

"Don't worry about it. Nobody has to know," he argued. "Rhody—the other night I got the impression you're on pretty good terms with Wright."

"He likes to get along with the press, yes."

"Good enough to drive past his gate guards?"

"Certainly." He could hear the nervousness in her voice. "I hunt and fish there often."

"That should do it." He calculated distances and driving times. "Get into some outdoors clothes. Come into town on Ocean Avenue and head up the valley road. I'll overtake you on the way."

"You've got a car?"

"Yeah, but I don't want to sit someplace and wait for you. See you in fifteen minutes." He hung up and went to Levine's car, took the chopper from the trunk and put it on the floor. He warmed the motor and turned north on a wide street.

He caught up with the Plymouth eight miles up the valley, flashed the spotlight at it. Rhody pulled over and he got in quickly, cradling the Thompson in his lap.

There was sudden fright in her eyes when she saw the machine gun. She wore tight jeans, an old leather jacket and boots and a visored cap was pulled over her hair. "Jensen ..."

"Drive," he ordered. "It only makes noise when you pull the trigger."

She drove. When they came to the place where he

was to meet Murdoch, there was nothing in sight in the clearing but a battered Jeep pickup truck with a canopy. He told her to park, then got out and walked toward the truck, cradling the Tommy gun in his arms. Softly he called, "Murdoch."

"In here, Jensen."

He went to the back end of the truck. The canopy flap was lifted and in the gloom he made out Captain Searle and Murdoch and two men in Highway Patrol uniforms. They were the ones who had arrested him and now they were staring at him like he was unreal.

"Jensen is the federal agent we've been waiting for. We're assisting him in a raid," Searle told his men.

They muttered exclamations of surprise as a police radio squawked.

"How's it look?" Jensen asked.

"We've got men on the gates, for what it's worth. Your boss is due in half an hour or so. He says to wait." A match flared and Searle puffed on a cigarette. "There's been some traffic in the last hour. I recognized Frank Lepage's car. He was in a hurry, and it looked like he had Dutchy Rohan with him. A few minutes later another car went up fast but we couldn't see who the guy was. A semi with a D-8 Cat on a lowboy went by too, if that means anything."

"I don't know," Jensen mused. "It may mean we don't have as much time as we hoped. Sounds like my busting out of jail got them shook and they've called a directors' meeting. They could be planning on using that dozer to close off the place. I'd better get rolling."

Murdoch looked around the edge of the flap and said, "Hey—that's Rhody's car!"

"Rhody's getting me in the gate. I promised her a big story."

"Oh, no," Murdoch protested. "You can't drag that girl into this thing. Jensen, there I draw the line."

"Relax. Once we're inside I'll bounce her out of the car. She won't be anywhere around."

"She better not be," Murdoch said firmly.

"Okay." Jensen handed the chopper to the nearest patrolman. "You might as well take this. Too clumsy."

He hurried to the convertible, got in the rear seat and said, "Make for the gate closest to the ranch house and do it fast!"

The car spun its wheels. When they were in sight of the gate he lay on the floor. He heard the horn blast twice, and then Rhody was talking to the gate guard. The car moved on, slower now, bumping over a graded dirt road. Jensen raised up. They were out of sight of the gate and he said, "Hold it here. I'll take it the rest of the way."

"No you don't, Jensen. You promised me a story," she retorted.

"You'll get it, Rhody. But I'm not heading for any picnic. It's damn well going to be dangerous."

"Just being near you is dangerous." She reached under the front seat, came up with a heavy revolver. "I brought this and believe me when I say I can shoot it if I have to. And listen—the gateman phoned ahead. They always do. If I don't check in at the ranch house, they'll figure something's up. They'd be looking to see what it is in no time."

"Can't argue with that. Roll this wagon and drop me off where the road circles behind the stables."

"What're you trying to do anyway?" she demanded. The car bumped ahead.

"Hang around close to the house and see who comes and goes for an hour or so. Keep them away from there if you can."

They passed the sprawling feed lot pens with their fat cattle and strong smells. The road climbed a small ridge and dipped into a bowl. Jensen could see the big ranch house and outbuildings and the first sun was hitting the forested peaks in the distance. Rhody braked the car with a barn between it and the house. "How's this?"

"Fine. Don't do anything foolish, Rhody." He got out.

She reached, caught him, pulled him down against her and kissed him suddenly, warmly. "I won't."

Then the car was gone and he was moving noiselessly through the half-light toward a door in the barn. He eased it open and stepped inside, into near-dark again. He could make out towering stacks of baled hay, some farm equipment, a pickup truck and jeep. The ignition key was in the jeep. He scouted around and saw there was no way to get it out of the barn without being seen from the house. Through a window he saw Rhody parking the car and walking toward the front door. There were several other cars in the parking area and he could see lights in several windows.

He prowled the barn, discovered a door leading to the attached stables. He could make out a dozen box stalls, and horses stamped and whinnied at the smell of him. He went through another door and found himself in a tack room. Saddles were racked along the walls and bridles hung neatly from pegs. He went to a window, saw about a hundred yards of open ground between the stables and a grove of oaks. The oaks grew thick on the hillside and would offer some concealment.

He grabbed a stout hackamore from the wall. There would be no time for a saddle. He went into the stable and found a likely-looking horse. It was black, with compact, chunky lines. He tossed the looped rope over the horse's neck, fitted the bosal to his nose, adjusted the head strap, opened the outer door. It had been years since he was on a horse and he had never ridden bareback. He seized the shaggy mane, leaped up and locked his legs firmly across the horse's chest.

The horse went. Jensen began to slide, caught himself and bent low. He recalled seeing television Indians doing it. The ground was soft but the drumming hooves made thunder in his ears. He didn't see how anyone within five miles could help but hear. He kept the outbuildings between himself and the ranch house and then he was in the oaks. He guided the horse up and over the rim of the bowl and slowed him to a trot until he could get his bearings. He decided the logging road he wanted should be more or less northerly from his position.

He found the road, saw tracks of a heavy truck. They were sharp and fresh. He followed the road until it became steep. The horse was lathered and Jensen could feel sweat soaking into his slacks. He reined up and listened.

From someplace nearby, he heard the sound of a heavy engine turning over at idling speed. He urged the horse ahead.

He saw the bulldozer when he had ridden another hundred yards. It squatted in a clearing. The tractor and lowboy trailer which had hauled it were nearby. There was no sign of a tunnel in the hillside. The slope was steep, covered with brush and scrub growth. Jensen knew the opening was there. Probably large, counterbalanced doors, built to hold a facade of earth and carefully planted with the vegetation of the surrounding terrain. He had seen similar installations at top-secret defense facilities.

A thin man in old work clothes leaned against the bulldozer. He was smoking a cigarette and he looked unhappy and sleepy.

Jensen debated with himself. With the 'dozer's diesel turning over, he could probably sneak up on the man through the brush. But the sun was well up now and he imagined one of two things would happen. Either Purvis would be on the scene, discover he had gone in alone and come after him or the boys doing the meanwhile-back-at-ranch bit might decide to see what he was doing back in hills.

He slipped the stubby .38 out and held it concealed in the horse's mane. Then he rode toward the bulldozer and tried to look like he belonged there. He was within fifty feet of the man before he looked up.

"Why the hell aren't you closing it off?" he snapped.

The man scowled as Jensen rode up and stopped the horse. "Because they ain't finished up, that's why."

"Then get your tail in and tell them to hump it," Jensen ordered. "There's cops all through these hills."

"Then to hell with it. I'm gettin' out." The man started for the truck. He turned suddenly, reaching for a pocket. His eyes fastened on Jensen's face and he yelled, "*Hey!*"

Jensen piled off the horse. His gun was pointed at the man's belly. "Federal officer," he snapped. "*Lift 'em.*"

The man raised his hands. Jensen slapped his pockets, found an automatic and tossed it into the brush. "Okay, buster. We're going in there. *Move!*"

He saw sudden fear in the red-rimmed eyes. "Not me! Not by—" The small man flinched and his eyes jerked to the right.

Jensen dropped fast and rolled as the shot was fired. He heard the 'dozer operator scream. The horse bolted at the second shot and Jensen fired blindly at the hillside, then crawled into the open long enough to grab the small man and drag him behind the big machine. The man was shaking, clutching his left shoulder where his jacket was torn. There was no blood. Jensen cuffed him and shouted, "Take me in there!"

"No'" His eyes rolled in his head and Jensen knew he was seeing blind terror. "He'd kill me before we got near it!"

Jensen swore at him. There had been no more shots and he thought there was a good chance that whoever had fired at him was doing something about looking for help. He scowled at the bulk of the bulldozer. It was a big rig, built for going through things.

"How do you make this thing go?" he demanded.

"Huh?" The operator looked at him as though he were mad.

"I want to drive it. Right through that damn mountain. You going to tell me how or get up there on the seat and do it for me?"

"You're crazy!"

"I'm mad. Figure out where that leaves you!"

"Okay. It looks like this." He drew lines in the dust with his finger. "Brakes here, one for each track. Two big levers are clutches. Shove 'em in, it goes ahead. Back toward you is reverse. Here's the throttle. Yank it out and leave it there. Transmission in the center. Pull it down to the left and you'll go like hell. Handle to the right of the seat runs the blade. Get it how high you want and twist the grip and it locks in place."

"That all?" Jensen's eyes were probing.

"All you gotta know."

"It better be. Because I'm cold-cocking you and putting you about three feet back of this beast. I wouldn't want to run over you."

"I wasn't lyin' … honest!"

Jensen hit him twice on the point of the chin. He dragged him well away from the throbbing machine and crawled up beside the track, studying the hillside carefully. He was able to make out faint tire marks in the dust. He looked for some sign of movement and calculated his chances of getting into the seat, swinging the big Cat around and raising the blade. Once he had that done, he might have a chance of staying alive.

He swallowed, shoved the gun in its holster, grabbed the edge of the seat and swung himself up. Before he hit the seat his right hand had found the throttle and slammed it through the quadrant and his left had knocked the transmission lever into a slot. He didn't take time to see which one. The tracks spun and the blade plowed dirt. He grabbed the blade control, pulled it until the thing came up high enough to offer some protection and threw both clutches forward. He ducked behind the protecting bulk of the motor, peeked around the left side, tried to follow the tire marks on the ground.

The diesel built up to an ear-splitting roar and he felt fierce beat. The face of the mountain didn't look like it was going to move even a little bit. There was a heavy steel canopy over the seat and Jensen wondered whether it would do any good.

He drove at full speed into the side of the mountain.

The grinding monster under him barely slowed. Stones and dirt and brush rained on him and he felt the right side of the blade hang up on something solid. He yanked both clutch levers back into his belly. The Cat shuddered to a halt, backed up. He headed it a little more to the left, threw the levers ahead again.

Metal screamed and broke and he was through, clanking down the concrete floor of a wide tunnel. Daylight streamed through the gaping hole behind him and there were bright lights in the tunnel roof. He cut the throttle back, saw the tractor would keep in a straight line unless he fooled with the controls and settled down to enjoy the ride. He had his gun out again and was nursing it around a curve to the left when the tunnel ended.

There was a cross-bore which he guessed followed the line of the old railroad. He could see hundreds of cardboard cartons stacked there. He decided it was time to get off. The Cat was barely moving. In another sixty feet it would be in the other tunnel. Whoever had shot at him earlier was probably waiting there, ready for him to ride up on his noisy yellow charger. He checked the line of travel, headed the Cat a little more to the right, opened the throttle wide again and jumped off the rear.

He ran for the side of the tunnel as the lumbering machine rammed the stacked cases. It plowed through them. Over the roar of the engine he could hear glass shattering. A pale brown river gushed from the mess. It smelled like bourbon.

The Cat bored ahead until the blade rammed the tunnel wall. It shuddered to a halt and spun its tracks in the slush of whisky and glass.

Jensen saw a man run down the tunnel and jump on the Cat. The motor stopped and for an instant the underground room was unnaturally quiet.

"Get off there with your hands up!" Jensen barked. He stepped from the entrance tunnel as the man on the tractor lifted his hands and turned slowly.

A big revolver hung on the man's thigh. Jensen jerked it away, stuck it under his belt.

"Hello, Shannon," he said.

McCullough Shannon lowered his hands slowly. There was a thin, mocking smile on his sharp face. The hawkish cast of his nose was heightened by the strip of tape across it.

CHAPTER 15

"Looks like I called it," Shannon said. "A federal."

"That's right."

"I got talked out of it for a while. A guy who's been around a long time said no T-man would bang around as clumsy as you."

"I'm dumb but stubborn." Jensen gestured with his gun. "I found this pot, didn't I?"

McCullough Shannon laughed softly. "You did at that. Now that you got it, what'll you do with it? Man, you got no chance at all to get off this place alive."

"That'll make two of us dead." Jensen found cigarettes and matches in his shirt pocket, tossed them to Shannon. "Light us a smoke."

"Crazy." Shannon got two cigarettes going. With his finger steady on the trigger Jensen took one, put it between his lips. Shannon blew smoke at him and said, "Now what?"

"First, you're under arrest on a charge of murdering a federal agent. Second, you're going to get on whatever passes for a house phone here and get Jim Wright and Lepage and the other rotten brains in this mess up for a drink or something. I want to talk to them." He waved the gun. "Let's get with it."

Shannon shrugged. He turned and walked a short distance down the main tunnel to a wall phone. He spun the dial.

"No tipoff or you've had it," Jensen said.

Shrugging, Shannon waited a moment, then said, "Jim. Better get up here fast and bring everybody. Got a hell of a mess on my hands ... goddamn Phil got loaded and ran the Cat right through the door ... yeah, the door. And right on down the hole and busted about two thousand cases. Yeah. And for Chrissakes bring that engineer. Discharge pipe is blocked and there's mash running all to hell. Yeah."

"That was good thinking," Jensen said as Shannon cradled the phone. "Now they won't be surprised about the door. Let's wander down where we can see them when they come."

"No. Let's see you drop the gun, Jensen." The voice was behind him, echoing in the tunnel.

Jensen started to turn. He froze and dropped the .38. Shannon stepped up, hit him in the stomach and in the same motion got his revolver from Jensen's belt. Jensen doubled over, clutched his belly. He waited for the killing smash on the back of his exposed head.

"*No, Cully!*" The other man was moving into the light. "We might need this one alive a little longer in case we have to bargain our way out."

Jensen stared at Oman Holbrook.

"You fingered Johnny," he said finally, in quiet hate. "You let this one kill him."

Jensen thought there was something sick and sad in the way the retired Treasury agent shook his head. "We knew who he was. Jensen, I'm the last one foolish enough to want what comes when a federal man is killed on a case. It was an—accident."

"I'll try to kill you in an accidental way too, Holbrook. And do the same for Shannon."

"Yeah, you will," Shannon muttered. "Why'd it take you so long to get a gun on this bird?"

"I was busy, remember? Emptying the pot all by myself isn't easy. Which reminds me—if I don't turn a valve or two soon it's bound to blow up and that will be the end of us." He gestured with the shotgun. "Jensen, as long as you looked so hard for this, I'm sure you'd enjoy a cook's tour. Cover him, Cully."

Shotgun across his elbow, Holbrook led the way toward the other end of the tunnel. They passed ceiling-high stacks of cases bearing the names of a score of whiskies, and then ranks of huge oak barrels, each neatly labeled. There was a faint hissing of steam ahead and then Jensen saw the still. He halted, felt grudging admiration for the builder.

It was set in a grotto blasted from the heart rock of the mountain, with a compact boiler and distillation column that poked upward through the roof of the stone-walled room. A cluster of gauges and valves filled a control panel. From the worm, a stainless-steel pipe was suspended over a barrel. Nothing flowed from the pipe. Five large vats were clustered at the other end, with more piping to carry the mash to the column. The vats were covered and there was almost no odor from whatever remained of the mash.

"Professional job," Jensen grunted. He realized the whole place was spotlessly clean. "You build it,

Holbrook?"

"Thank you," the old man said in a soft voice. "I only designed it. I couldn't connect up the pipes for a bathtub. But it makes excellent whisky."

"So our lab report said," Jensen replied in a dry tone. "I suppose Wright's cows covered you on buying grain and the like."

Holbrook was pressing switches and turning valves. Jensen heard water surge through pipes. "Mister Wright is in a position to provide everything. He even turned up a nice little natural gas well so we can have a fire."

"How long you gonna yap at this guy?" Shannon demanded.

"A little conversation will help pass the time until the others get here," Holbrook said mildly. "Incidentally, Jensen, they know you're here. I'm the engineer Cully asked them to bring. As a matter of fact, Cully and I expected you. I talked with the house just before you arrived so noisily and was told someone stole one of Mister Wright's horses just after the Cranston girl arrived. A coincidence?"

"That bitch—" Shannon began.

"Why, Cully, she's a lovely girl," Holbrook said mockingly. "I remember the day you'd have done anything in the world for—"

"*Shut up, you yammering goat!*" Shannon barked. "Do whatever you have to do to this teakettle and shut up."

Holbrook chuckled and turned a handle. A grayish

fluid drained from the base of the boiler and swirled down a hole in the flooring. "Really an ideal location, Jensen. Column fits just fine inside the old mine shaft and we have a nice little underground stream to give us water and carry the waste off. Well-filtered by the time it shows up above ground."

Jensen was puzzled. From the expression on Holbrook's face he couldn't tell whether he was serious or having a quiet joke; proud of what he had built or ashamed of his part in it.

"Why?" he asked finally. "Any reason?"

"No reason that would appear justified to you, Mister Jensen," Holbrook said after a moment's thought. "But suppose you had worked forty years on a job and when you left you got a gold watch and two hundred dollars a month. A dog can't live on that. Not today."

"That Blind Pig of yours looked prosperous."

"Oh, it is. It makes a little money. But I spent more years than you've lived dealing with noisy drunks in one way or another." He shook his head. "At that, I had to borrow what it took to get started. No, I guess I just didn't want to die on my feet pouring liquor by the shot. There's more fun to making it by the barrel— particularly when you were on the other side so long."

"I'm sorry," Jensen said quietly. "I'm sorry you see it that way."

Holbrook shrugged in a futile way. There was a grinding sound in the distance and the sound of a motor filled the tunnel. Holbrook picked up his shotgun and Shannon herded Jensen back the way they had come.

A car, moving at high speed, shot from the entrance tunnel into the main bore. It was the Plymouth convertible, the top down now. Frank Lepage drove. Jim Wright was on the right side, a heavy automatic in his hand. Dutchy Rohan rode in back, and he had a pump shotgun.

As the car skidded and spun around in the spilled liquor and broken glass, Jensen saw the white, scared face of Rhody Cranston in the middle of the front seat.

Wright got out. He stood with gun lowered and viewed the wreckage around the bulldozer. As if he expected a reasonable answer, he asked Jensen, "Now why did you have to do something like that?"

"I wanted to get in and I was being shot at."

Wright walked around in the broken glass, kicking it with the pointed toes of his boots. He saw a bottle that had survived. He raised the gun, shot the neck off it and slipped the gun into his pocket.

Frank Lepage got out of the car. He held Rhody by the elbow. She was staring at Shannon with a look Jensen couldn't interpret.

"What's the matter, little cat?" Shannon said to her. "You think I went over with the car?"

She said nothing.

"Well, Jensen," Wright said. "Let's get to it. I don't suppose you came alone."

"There are others." Jensen began to understand how Wright had stayed on top in the rackets for a quarter of a century. The man was intelligent enough to consider what was going against him and not overestimate a temporary advantage. "They should be here any minute."

"I wonder what kind of a deal we can make."

"We don't have to deal with this guy," Shannon said. "We got him, haven't we?"

"Shut up, Cully," Wright said quietly.

"I won't even talk about a deal with Rhody here," Jensen said. "Let her get in that car and go and then we'll see."

"No, no, we couldn't do that." Wright eyed the girl, chuckling. "She might bring your men back too soon."

Rhody's fingers toyed with the zipper of her jacket. She met Jensen's eyes and said, "I'll stay."

Jensen sighed. "Then I'll level with you. There's no deal I can make. If you hand over your guns and surrender I'll mention it to the U. S. attorney when the case comes up."

"Jim—we could take him with us and make a run," Lepage said hopefully. "They wouldn't blast us with him in the car."

"You've already killed one agent," Jensen said. "My boss would figure I was as good as dead. They'd shoot, and they're good enough to miss me."

"But I wouldn't," Shannon told him. There was impatient fire in his black eyes.

They stood in a rough circle, warily eyeing each other. Rhody was to Jensen's left, Shannon a few feet to his right. Holbrook was almost directly opposite Jensen, with Wright and Lepage to his left. Dutchy

Rohan was by the car watching the ragged tunnel entrance.

Jensen thought about the gun Rhody had put under the seat. If it was still there, and if he could somehow get to the car, they had a chance.

He studied McCullough Shannon. Shannon was not a waiter. He was good in action, but he could not wait.

"You might come out better than you think, Wright," Jensen said thoughtfully. "All except Shannon."

"Just what's …" Shannon began.

Wright silenced him with a glance. "How's that?"

"Shannon killed our man Levangie. He's a sure bet for the gas house." He paused, took his time getting a cigarette lighted. "Maybe that was a personal thing, over the girl. Levangie was making it with her. She's not too hard to get but she could be hard to get over …" He saw color in her face and her eyes flared from him to Shannon. "So. If that was something he did on his own, and you can put a reasonable argument that you didn't have any part of it, well …"

A whisper of a laugh came through Wright's lips. "Well what, Jensen?"

"The worst you can expect is pulling a few years for making booze. You can afford lawyers; it shouldn't be too many." He sucked on the cigarette. "And it beats a gassing."

"How about it, Cully?" Wright said mockingly. "Want to make a grand gesture?"

Shannon raised the .44, swung it in a half circle. "Any more talk like that and you won't have to worry about doing any time. None at all."

Rhody Cranston shut her eyes and hugged herself inside the old leather jacket.

Jensen realized Oman Holbrook was staring steadily at him. Their eyes met and he saw Holbrook's throat move as he swallowed. Jensen saw the twin muzzles of the shotgun move slightly in Shannon's direction.

"A man who sells out once finds it easier the second time," Holbrook said matter-of-factly. "Put the guns down."

The sound of guns was sudden, deafening.

From the hip, Shannon fired once at Holbrook. The old man stumbled back and blood spurted from his throat. His knees buckled as his finger tightened on the double triggers in a spasm of pain.

The charge of buckshot struck Jim Wright in the chest when his automatic was half out of his pocket.

Jensen jumped Cully Shannon as the hawk-faced man brought his gun around, caught his wrist. The fingers of Jensen's right hand hit the wrist bones like a cleaver. He heard Shannon yell as the big gun dropped.

From the corner of his eye Jensen saw Rhody Cranston's hand dip inside the jacket, come out with the gun she had showed him in the car.

Dutchy Rohan was running around the back of the convertible, working the slide of the pump gun when she fired. The heavy slug tore the front of Rohan's head off.

Rhody's hand flew shoulder-high and recoil kicked

the gun from her hand. It hit the floor and bounced away. Jensen hung on as Shannon braced himself and tried to tear free. Their flailing feet kicked Shannon's gun toward Rhody.

She grabbed it as Lepage, apparently frozen by the sudden violence, reached under his coat. She fired once. The slug punched through the fat man's shirt where the third button had been. He spun around with the impact. The gun made its howitzer sound again and a black hole appeared in the gray hair at Lepage's temple. The barrel had jerked only a couple of inches with each shot.

Jensen stepped in close to Shannon and drove his right fist into the big man's midsection. It was like hitting a tree, but the force of the blow hurled Shannon away from him.

Shannon stumbled back through shards of glass and piled into the rear of the bulldozer. He straightened. Jensen saw his left hand close on the heavy drawbar safety chain.

Shannon yanked at the chain, trying to throw it at Jensen. The end was still shackled to the tractor and it tore from his grasp. Off balance, he floundered toward Jensen. He said something that was lost in the crash of a case of whisky on the floor.

The howitzer went off again. Jensen saw Rhody beside him, her face twisted in fury. The bullet hit just above Shannon's belt buckle. The impact jackknifed him forward. Without seeming to aim, she hit him in the head with the second shot.

Before she could fire again, Jensen caught the gun by the cylinder, twisted it from her hand. She screamed and turned on him, clawing his face.

He hit her with the palm of his hand and she screamed one more time, then fell against him, burying her face in the hollow of his shoulder. He stroked her back until she seemed to be under control.

"Come on," he said gently. "You want to get out of here."

He picked up the gun she had dropped. Her eyes followed him without seeming to recognize him as he went to each of the others. They were all dead. He found his gun in Shannon's hip pocket, and his eyes passed over the dozen or so fresh shells in the loops of the dead man's gun belt.

He put his arm across the girl's shoulder, turned her around and they walked down the tunnel to the ragged daylight.

CHAPTER 16

They came in three cars and two pickup trucks, and they carried rifles and submachine guns and tear gas grenades; enough to wage a small war. Jensen and Rhody sat on the lowboy trailer and waited for them to arrive.

Purvis and Captain Searle and Brud Cousins were in the lead car. They skidded to a stop in the dust and Jensen waved wearily with a hand that still held a .44 Magnum.

"Inside. They killed each other off," he said.

"How'd you come out?" Purvis asked.

Jensen shook his head. "Alive. A little gun-shy."

"We'll take a look." Purvis started to move away but Jensen motioned him back.

"Holbrook was in it too. When he saw it was all over he tried to come back."

Purvis' face became rigid. "I'll talk it over with you later, Kon."

They went away. Jensen looked at the two big pistols, at the golden-haired woman beside him. The signs of crying were already leaving her face; she still managed to be spectacular.

"I'll give you something," he said. "With the right gun in your hand, you can sure shoot."

"Kon—I don't want to talk about it."

He watched her hands lace and unlace in her lap.

"Better if you do. Or so the doctor's say. Talk it out of you."

He examined the guns. Both were Smith and Wesson, with *.44 Magnum* engraved on the barrels. "Take this one you managed to sneak in there." He fit it into her unwilling right hand. "Nice, but they didn't measure you right when they made those custom grips. Look—you've got a small hand. Can't close it over the butt and still reach the trigger."

She put the gun down, not looking at it. Jensen took it, ejected the shells and put them in his pocket. He closed her fingers around the one Shannon had used to kill Oman Holbrook.

"Now this looks like a better fit, Rhody. See the way it sits in your palm and gives you plenty of trigger finger."

"Jensen!" Her voice was sharp, near hysteria again. "Damn it, I don't want to ever—"

"Don't want to be gun-shy the rest of your life, do you?" he said, unperturbed. "Now like I was saying, this cannon of Shannon's would be better for you than your own." He took a cartridge from his pocket. "You had full Magnum loads in that little gem. Armor-piercing, at that. No wonder it bucked right out of your hand the first shot."

"What're you after?" she said angrily. She tried to throw Shannon's gun away but Jensen kept her hand closed on it.

"Just trying to tell you a little about guns. Now you look here. Shannon was a cop of sorts but he didn't have bullets built to go through a tank. Cousins said the one he killed Johnny with was an underpowered standard .44. No more kick to it than a .38. And this thing says .44 Magnum, but take a look at the cylinder. Been changed over for standard .44's. Couldn't even put a Magnum shell in there."

"Jensen! I don't *care*—"

"Funny guy to figure out, Shannon. Some of the things he did don't make sense at all. Like him carrying around a gun belt loaded with Magnum shells when his gun wouldn't take them. And a man with hands as big as his could handle lot bigger grips than those on the gun you've got in your hand."

The color had drained from her face. The morning was warm but he felt her shiver.

"Contrary sort, but I guess he loved you. He must have if he was willing to take a chance on a murder rap for you."

"*You*—" Before he could move she had twisted and jammed the muzzle of the gun against his ribs.

He swallowed hard, looked deep into the piercing eyes that could be so soft.

"With all these cops around, Rhody?" he said calmly. "You'd never beat it then."

She shut her eyes and the beautiful mouth trembled.

He took it from her gently, because he was afraid not to be gentle. "I'd already unloaded it, Rhody."

"You were Shannon's woman. You were also a set of ears for the boys. Anything brewing in town that could be bad news, you'd pick up a rumble at the *Globe*.

Holbrook knew Levangie, so you made yourself—pleasant. I suppose Johnny tied you in and you didn't like the thought of doing time instead of having a nice piece of side money coming in. Knowing Johnny, I suppose he gave you a chance to get out, maybe turn state's evidence." He got a cigarette going. "For this you shot him in the back. You called Shannon, and Shannon fixed it all up. Idiot was willing to cover for you, but he had to trade you guns. No wonder you wanted to stay in there with me. You knew if a deal was made, you'd be in the pot. That about it?"

She looked at him. There was nothing behind the gray eyes now. She was a shell, a beautiful, empty shell.

Jensen waved a plainclothesman over. "Cuff her and take her in."

A mortuary wagon was removing the bodies. Purvis heard Jensen's report and swore softly.

"We'd have been here a lot quicker but we thought they were trying to hotfoot it out a back road. We didn't know where you'd gone until we heard all that racket."

"Just as good. I'd have been shot for sure if anyone came down that tunnel." Jensen realized he was bone-tired now that his work was done.

"We've got a lot of people. It will take some time to sort them all out."

"Spare me that. I'll turn in sick if I have to interrogate anybody."

"Your fellow escapee Mayo is back in jail," Purvis said. "He turned himself in because he didn't feel like running the rest of his life."

"He's a good guy. I'd like to see him get a new trial." Jensen stood, stretched, yawned at the sun. "I'm going."

"Yes?"

"There is a girl with dark red hair and green eyes and an Irish temper that's nothing but mean at five-thirty in the A.M." He looked at the sun. "It must be about eleven now. I'll go see if it makes a difference."

THE END

Jay Flynn was born John M. Flynn on March 31, 1928, in Massachusetts. A hard-drinking Boston Irishman, he worked variously as a newspaperman, a bartender, editor, sex novelist, bootlegger, security guard, caretaker and, he claimed, "writer-in-residence" at a Nevada whorehouse. His first published work was his only short story, "The Badger Game," followed by the novel, *The Deadly Boodle* as J. M. Flynn, part of an Ace Double in 1958. In 1975, Flynn went to work for the low-tier publisher, Belmont-Tower, where he lasted two years—fired because of his drinking—then moved to Richmond, Virginia, where he lived for a while on skid row. Eventually relocating to Connecticut, he checked into a V.A. hospital in Branford for a checkup, where he died of cancer at age 57 on February 6, 1986.

Jay Flynn Bibliography
(1927-1985)

As J. M. Flynn:

The Deadly Boodle (Ace
Double D-313, 1958)
Drink with the Dead (Ace
Double D-379, 1959)
Terror Tournament
(Mystery House
[hardcover], 1959; Ace
Double D-409 [paperback
reprint, abridged], 1959)
The Hot Chariot (Ace
Double D-447, 1960)
Ring Around a Rogue (Ace
Double D-459, 1960)
One for the Death House
(Ace Double D-511, 1961)
The Girl from Las Vegas
(Ace Double F-111, 1961)
Deep Six (Ace Double F-
125, 1961)
The Screaming Cargo (Ace
Double F-130, 1962)
SurfSide 6 (Dell 8388; TV
tie-in, 1962)
Assault No. 1: The Raid on
Reichswald Fortress
(Award, 1974)
Warlock (Pocket Books
80478, 1976)
Danger Zone (Belmont-
Tower 51171, 1977;
reprinted in Australia as
Jet Set Orgy, Stag, 1979)

As Jay Flynn [McH =
McHugh. JR = Joe Rigg.
B = Bannerman]

McHugh (Avon T-377, 1959)
McH
It's Murder, McHugh (Avon
T-406, 1960) McH
A Body for McHugh (Avon
T-444, 1960) McH
Viva McHugh (Avon T-466,
1960) McH
The Action Man (Avon T-
500, 1961)
The Five Faces of Murder
(Avon F-156; 1962) McH
Blood on Frisco Bay
(Leisure 360, 1976) JR
Trouble Is My Business
(Leisure 384, 1976) JR
Bannerman (Leisure 389,
1976) B
Border Incident (Leisure,
1976) B

Western novels:

As Jack Slade/Lassiter
series:

Lust for Gold (Belmont-
Tower 51127, 1977)
Hangman (Belmont-Tower
51146, 1977)
Wolverine (Belmont-Tower
51225, 1978)

Short story:
"The Badger Game," as by
Jay Flynn (Guilty
Detective Story Magazine,
Nov. 1956)

www.ingramcontent.com/pod-product-compliance
Lightning Source LLC
Chambersburg PA
CBHW061256120726

48001CB00001B/335